THE CHESTERFIELD HOURS

THE CHESTERFIELD HOURS

THE

CHESTERFIELD

HOURS

Gwyn Parry

To Matt — Good travel reading, I hope and trust.

Once Upon Avon Press

David Dauschel ("GP")

Canandaigua   New York

THE CHESTERFIELD HOURS

THE CHESTERFIELD HOURS is a work of fiction, and the usual
rules apply. I am not I, you not he or she, they not them.
It, on the other hand, is what it is.

THE CHESTERFIELD HOURS

In memory of my real Victoria, a beauty and nobody's granny

THE CHESTERFIELD HOURS

THE CHESTERFIELD HOURS

CONTENTS

THE CHESTERFIELD HOURS

THE CHESTERFIELD HOURS

THEY MADE ME

I suppose the first air I ever breathed was filled with her voice. But even in the agony of childbirth, she'd not have broken form:

"I came through the Blitz as a child, darling boy. What had I to fear from the rubs and scrapes of little you?"

Fair enough. But speaking of war and all that, why don't I sound like my father Jack, the fightingest blood and guts Marine of his day?

(He'd have made colonel on battlefield promotions alone, an old ranker once told me, if it weren't for the little matter of the general's wife.)

"Make that generals' wives, dear."

For better or worse, England and America made me, and we are all Americans now. So WTF, today's American reader may ask, who is this bloke, er, dude, and why does he talk like that?

I'd say it's because Captain Jack Chesterfield was always in strange lands and strange beds, while Daphne Ffoulkes Chesterfield spoke the language and ethic that I breathed in:

"There never was a time like good King Edward's, dear. For fun, for peace, and for talk. It was Shakespeare and Elizabeth with proper drains and no bear-baiting."

That would be 1910, if you're wondering. Not 1400, or 1066. Understand, my mother never saw any of those years, though she'll surely see 3000 in her present... state.

THE CHESTERFIELD HOURS

What a mad pair, Jack and Daphne, but they made me. And what did they give "little me" that figures in our story?

Laughter. Guts. Fidelity. Ironic, that last one, as my Leatherneck dad had such trouble, domestically, with the *Semper* part.

"'Tis not a year or two shows us a man.' So thank God for good bourbon."

Laughter, guts, fidelity. What are they worth today? Quite a lot, by the timeless measure of supply/demand. And what's in heavy supply? Sad to report, it's all between these covers: adulterous rumpy-pumpy, shameless gold-digging, cyber-fraud, steroid-juiced thuggery, rampant under-the-bus-throwing...

And I just a young gentleman schoolteacher who's having none of it.

But I've said forever, it's the women who'll save us. Read on, and meet the smashingest girl ever, name of Carrie Hahn, and the stellar dog Daisy, who sniffs out villains a mile away, and the lioness-hearted "gym-chick" Jeanine, who carried the day when I fell wounded, and who made a man of my gormless pal Larry.

And yes, the fair sex throws a wrong 'un from time to time, like the alluring fortune-huntress name of Deborah, a wily adversary who passed for a while as my wife.

But it's the mum who made me –

"Well, who else? I mean, have you got your brain on?"

-- and she gets our story's final word, from Heaven, or someplace.

Right. In the end, I couldn't have done it without her... ghost.

THE CHESTERFIELD HOURS

Book One

CHESTERFIELD GETS THE GATE

Part One

THAT'LL DO, DAISY

Things were swimming along, I thought, in the January of that recent year. My beloved parents Jack and Daphne, and my corgi dog Daisy, were all in super fettle. I was molding, day by day, a promising batch of sixth-graders, excepting always the dead-ender Dylan Czarnecki. And I was married to a bright and beautiful woman – six years in now, without an itch. My and Deborah's little Cape-style house had been our peaceable domain.

If only the larger metropolis were so peaceable. One brisk Saturday that month, I was jogging Daisy through the city park when the pooch picked up on two voices from off the path.

Well, Daisy always knows. A big pratting bully of a fellow, in an over-sized "hoodie," was raging at a young woman leashed to a tiny, cowering terrier.

"You lyin' ----!" the hulking young man bellowed. I'll usually give you letter one of a bad word – but not that one.

"I say."

The young man jerked round at me. With hands in the hoodie's uni-pocket, he said, "Who the f--- are you?" There's a letter you can work with.

I moved closer. Woman and terrier looked tensed to flee.

"Step away so we can sort you out," I told the bully, and gently jingled Daisy's leash.

Something immense moved under the young man's sweatshirt, in the uni-pocket. Like a weekend gangster he pulled a monstrous piece of metal and trained it on me.

"M----------r," he said, "this is a Sig Sauer." Just the fiendish sort of cannon Germans stay up late making.

Couldn't call it easy on the nerves. But what did old Winston say is our aim, against naked aggression? In a word, victory. And our policy?

"Well then," I said, "this is a dog. Daisy, go to!"

My corgi launched herself upwards into the vandal's groin area, knocking up his gun arm. I caught that arm and swept one leg behind the man's legs, simultaneously yanking him to the pavement and dislocating arm and shoulder. The weapon clattered onto the path. The hooligan shrieked, but boo bloody hoo, he made this grotty business...

And getting grottier, as Daisy sank her fangs into...

"Aieaarrgh! Oh mother!"

"Daisy, stand easy!"

Woman and terrier had vanished. A pity, since His Bullyness was nicely teed up for her to blast a Jimmy Choo into his man-tonsils. Why should Daisy have all the fun?

I had a wash to do, and wanted breakfast, so the urge was strong to leave the hooded debris like a cast-off sack of doggy poo. But duty to the general welfare impinged, as it always does upon the gentleman. I took charge of the weapon and called the police who, doubtless well-breakfasted, arrived thereafter.

THE CHESTERFIELD HOURS

CHESTERFIELD GETS THE GATE

So there would be skirmishes. That is our life, even for the fortunate. And one *is* fortunate for home, hearth, trusty dog... and a wife who's a walking Anglican hymn: all things bright and beautiful, you know. I put Daisy in the front seat so I could stroke and praise her. With no harm done in the park, Deborah would get a smile out of her "little girl's" feats.

Right, Daisy's the tough guy, not I. Likewise hoodie-hooligan would have cheesed at one hard look from my dad, a thirty-year retired Marine. For my part I try to honor my British mum's teachings. Loads of fun, she is, but positively feudal. A gentleman does... a gentleman does NOT... That's benign authority, in her book.

Works for villains, not massively well for wives, as we'll see...

We arrived home to find Deborah's car out of the garage, its trunk open.

Daisy, no leash on her, hopped right out and ran to the front door. When I opened it and stepped through, Deborah stood there day-elegant in dress wool slacks, blouse and herringbone blazer. She had beside her a travel case with wheels on it.

"Oh," she said.

"Right," I said. Daisy sniffed about Deborah's dress boots as if rodents had bred there.

"When you didn't come back right away," she said, "I figured you went on and did the shopping."

"Ah," was all I said – still groping, what?

She took this, I think, as my torturing out of her the old deep and dark, as when the coppers clam up and let a mouthy crook hang himself. Anyway she got quite shirty, quite quickly.

"Listen, it's not working," she said and, taking up her wheely case, strode to the door. Daisy just sat glass-eyed.

"What not working, that bloody loo flush again?" I said – lightening things a bit, you know. "Don't let it get to you, love."

Came a cropper. She was out the door, her boots clicking on the driveway as I stood in the lurch. Does a gentleman run after, wrestle with doors, lie under tires? No to all. Some retire to the library and blow their brains out, under certain conditional standards of propriety. But I lacked the library, the gun, the mood really. Yet I can't say I felt quite the full ticket. Six lovely years, then one rummy morning...

THE CHESTERFIELD HOURS

SUNDAY

So what's a gentleman to do, with a bolter on his hands?

For now, I thought, let's keep it inside the family.

"I mean to say, darling boy," my mother Daphne said as she handed me a plate of poached and bangers, "it's the truly virile man that a woman must flee in the end."

"I'd have liked one last shot at Deborah," my father Jack, a dedicated lifelong chaser, said ruefully from the kitchen table. "I always thought if I bided my time that eventually she'd come to me with the goods."

"Oh, what a lot of rot you talk, Jack." My mother waved dismissively at him. As she did so, her one bit of posh, an ancient family ring of diamonds and sapphires, glinted in harmony with her morning blue kimono.

"Well, Dad," I said, "*allez cherchez*." It was just the morning after Deborah left on "vacation," dragging that one suitcase on little hot wheels.

My guv'nor Captain Jack, sixty-six, gray and brawny with a Marine globe and anchor tattooed to his forearm, mused, "Your mother could take her own vacation with young Ben Hoepplewhite, I suppose. I wouldn't stand in the way."

"Oh, tosh," mum Daphne said. "Have you noticed Ben's calf muscles, though, when he wears those really long shorts and Blucher moccasins?"

17

THE CHESTERFIELD HOURS

Benedict Hoepplewhite, mortgage broker and born prole, was riding high these days, owing to refi madness. My and Deborah's Cape Cod, purchased rather witlessly at peaks in price and rate, had brought him buzzing round yet again.

"Well, Mother," I said, "I'd have you go and do your bewitching worst, if it kept him away from Deb... say, when did you last see Hoepplewhite?"

Daphne cast me one of her lascivious smiles.

"My dear, you're streets ahead of him in the hot-stuff department. At most she'd need him for a little soft currency after your six years' onslaught." She glanced at the randy old guv'nor. "God knows I understand that."

***

The Mum's belief in my alleged ravening potency was as firm as it was mortifying. But Deborah's move was, I knew, a ruthlessly practical one. My prospects were capped. Of money I had little. I, Chesterfield, was a shanty WASP.

Now what, then? From Jack, I inherited a body useful and willing. And from Daphne? A gentleman's ethic in which I still believed -- and a rumoured family fortune, in which I couldn't, quite.

That's because I'd only come into it as a geezer, if ever. Daphne still hadn't a farthing to show. Granny Victoria, now ninety-one, would have gained the lot at age seventy-three. No one knew how much. The Ffoulkes bred one child to a generation, and lived excruciatingly long. They married gold-digging cads and huntresses who died or departed after too many years of the stick with no carrot, no pot at rainbow's end...

THE CHESTERFIELD HOURS

Captain Jack Chesterfield was the better sort of Ffoulkes mate, Daphne would say after two Manhattans, as he'd stuck it thirty-eight years now with resort to only three of her girl cousins and at most six of her friends.

Beyond doubt, and for the worse, the world was speeding up. Thus Deborah had cut losses and chucked it, at the tender age of thirty-one. The Fortune was nothing to me, but marriage and honor were much. I would begin inquiries into friend Hoepplewhite.

JEANINE AND THE JOYS OF SPINNING

"Whaddaya need, hon?"

I'd just stepped inside Ripped & Shredded, the gymnasium to which Deborah, and Hoepplewhite, belonged. A quite muscular, belatedly blonde young lady addressed me from the doorway to a darkened room, from which issued a crashing din of recorded bass-driven noise, flashing light, and live human shrieks.

"Oh, hello there," I said, faking nonchalance. "Name's Chesterfield. I've been round a few times, picking up my wife who's one of your members. Is she about?"

"Deborah?"

"Right." As the woman caught me staring at her exposed midsection, I felt myself redden. She had a biggish steel missile plunged through her navel, and a crimson and blue illustration radiating outward across the abdomen, suggesting a casualty on some pagan battlefield.

"Not in a couple days, hon," the woman said. "Usually she's every day."

"Ah," I said. "I guess she's got us both at sea." I stepped toward the darkened room in a kind of fascination.

The woman yielded slightly as I peeked in. Harrowing scene, Dantesque even. Five figures thrashed furiously on bicycles, as light strobed over them and the noise crashed away. One figure, female, wore a wireless microphone and screamed incomprehensible commands to the

20

others, whose tortured eyes glinted from out of the shadows. Their acute agonies, the cruel searching light and exploding barrage struck me as a trench raid tableau from the Great War.

"Spinning class," the woman yelled in my ear. "You oughta try it some time."

Do you like seeing any woman sweat like a very hog? I didn't, though I realized times had changed. Among the five dripping and spastic figures was a single male, who seemed to me infinitely pathetic.

"I say," I said to the woman. "I wonder if our pal, Benedict Hoepplewhite, is pitching it here today."

"Ben's your friend?" she said. "He's such a hottie. Tell him I said that."

I gritted out a smile. "Not on the premises, then, I take it."

A wad of blue gum showed in her teeth as she stopped chewing to ponder.

"Now that you mention it," she said, "he's usually every day too. But I think he's away."

I thanked her and turned to go.

"Tell Ben what I said," the woman said. "It's better when it's a third person, you know?"

I turned back round. "Devilishly subtle," I said. "Who should I say called him a hottie?"

"Jeanine at R & S."

"Righto."

THE CHESTERFIELD HOURS

THE FORTUNE AND THE FATAL THIRD ONE

I taught sixth grade because its requirements were precisely myself.
What gentleman doesn't like a job with a proper lunch and a bit of sport in
the middle? I fancied I was surely the best kickball player in the world, as
I'd been at it twenty-five years.

I liked children and, in the spare Ffoulkes tradition, hoped to have
one of my own some day. Sixth grade fit the bill, since a male there
induced no parental abdabs as with, say, kindergarten. And a sixth-grader
was not yet the stinking beast he would become once I'd shoved him
onward to junior high. It had worked out pretty well…

"Darcy is a f-----' ho!" exclaimed Dylan Czarnecki, as his antagonist
plated the winning run for the girls' team.

Gendered competitions were very bitter now. I called for the ball.

"Line up!" I said. "Dylan will lunch with me in the room."

"Aw!" As it was winter, we played in the gym.

The world was speeding up. Dylan's precocious little oath returned
me to my own plight. In a better world, say Shakespeare's, it was no sin to
decide that one's wife was a dollymop. Naturally one concluded it silently
– one did not proclaim it.

But I wouldn't yet conclude it of Deborah, not without proof.

What if she wanted better than a Honda and a Cape Cod? And what
dirty fellow would lay her a slime-trail of gilt promises, sneering

comparisons of income, and his own revolting footprints, tracking back into my little castle?

Hoepplewhite's merest scent was tangible compared to The Ffoulkes Fortune, of which I'd caught not a whiff in my thirty-two years. Now, once you suspect your spouse of playing away from home, you'll straightaway reflect on his or her recent behavior. I did so, and embarrassing to say, found a root implicating not only Deborah but my own mother. Inconvenient, as I'd already in my own mind called out and killed Hoepplewhite. But there it was.

Call it The Night of the Third Manhattan.

Daphne had three at our rehearsal dinner. It was the groom's parents' party and their choices were superb. It was a fall wedding, and the University Club produced an excellent dinner of squab, root vegetables sweetened and pounded to mush, and French wine. It far exceeded any party you'd expect from pensioners, and Jack at least took the kudos in his stride. Daphne glided like a sylph through the cocktail hour on one Manhattan; capped her second during dinner with a languorous touch of the bride's father's hand; and once in possession of the fatal third took Deborah arm in arm to a divan in the smoking room.

There, more came out pertaining to The Fortune than in the lifetimes of me and father Jack combined. As to how much the tipsy Daphne embellished, and how deeply the materialist Deborah probed, no gentleman would ask.

But The Fortune had thus dwelt with us from Day One Minus One, to myself as an abstraction, to Deborah as perhaps more. Frequently she would allude to it, in early days as a kind of benevolent uncle, more lately as an adverse and sadistic Scrooge. Then, over the past several months, silence. A less golden attendant of this last period had been Hoepplewhite, in his new incarnation as preening success, bashing us over the heads with the need to "refi." He and Deborah spent pleasant workday noons, flipping through his rate books over cappuccino lunches.

These she leapt to justify by floating Hoepplewhite's further insulting suggestion that Jack and Daphne do with him a reverse mortgage, to enjoy a greater income until...

Well, to me there was no "until." The Fortune would be there, or not. I would retire a teacher of thirty years. Of course no gentleman lets the state provide for him, but as I saw it the teacher's pension was simply the return of my own, less an unfortunate haircut for the bungling of bureaucratic managers. In the meantime, there was our cozy house and its books, the pleasures of sport and nature, our Daisy, our intimacy...

No decent narrative, of course, expatiates on such intimacy. Whilst they are married a couple's relations must be satisfactory. If those relations were not satisfactory, the couple would not be married...

"Do you mind telling me," demanded Deborah a few weeks before she left, as she sat at her computer, "Do you mind telling me why there's an email here with the subject line "Get a better h---on?"

"Good God!"

"Well?"

My school colleague Larry Berkowitz said he'd been blitzed with icky solicitations for gender- and age-inappropriate pharmaceuticals. I had only the vaguest as to what was "spam" and what a "pop-up"; I only knew that if these terms had been separated from soldiers and baseball, it was a poor world indeed.

THE CHESTERFIELD HOURS

"Have I not told you," I said to Deborah, "that electronic mail is the end of civil society?" The comma splices, the run-ons, the no caps, the all caps, the !!!

"Well," my wife replied with a strained hauteur, "*I'm* not looking for a better h---on. You must be getting on here and not telling me."

"I am getting on nowhere. It's your infernal contraption and welcome to it. It's amusing these new-age brilliant fellows can't grasp Marketing 101. Know your customer and all that. What that customer's actual parts are, and aren't -- "

"Okay!"

Looking back, I hated to think that Deborah, so lovely and generous, would pick a fight just to make me feel unworthy or guilty. What did the old Viennese witch doctor -- as Nabokov called Freud -- say about projection?

But a lady is presumed innocent. First I'd look to that mortgage-hawking swine...

THE CHESTERFIELD HOURS

NEW MEANS FOR OLD MISCHIEF

One trip to the gym was enough conventional tracking. I'm an old-fashioned sort of a lad – have you noticed? – but I decided that new-age detection was wanted now. Wouldn't you, if your best pal was a bloody genius with the old "infernal contraption"?

"I can create a new domain from here," Larry Berkowitz said. "Make it look like one of those crazy ones the ads come from."

We sat in his tech lab at school. Larry and I get on well because he doesn't take me for something next-door to a butler, as many will do. And I don't view him, as others do, merely through his biggest lack – of the social graces, that is. I mean to say, ladies, if the mind is the true erogenous zone, he's your fella, what?

I asked, "Isn't there always an actual name as well as address and subject line?"

"How about mine? It's easy, it's honest, and to this slob who did your wife, it's just a name. These things are always from some ordinary-sounding stranger – "

"Brilliant! You're a pal."

" -- or else they're from Bambi, or Tif -- "

"Or Jeanine."

The door swung behind us with a squeal, and sickly hallway light oozed into the lab. Fay Muck, the building principal, stood in the doorway.

"Why, Mister Chesterfield. I thought I'd see the pearly gates before I saw you at a computer."

"Why, Ms. Muck," I said ambiguously, "no one deserves a more straightaway passage through those gates than your splendid self. But there you have me. A computer to me is only a tea tray."

She edged inwards toward us. She was an edgy sort of a girl, you'll see.

"So where's the tea?" she said in her nasal alto-tenor.

Worthy adversaries, I always considered us. Like Holmes and Moriarty but affectionate, almost. Larry, though, was jumpy and fearful of her. Still wanting sophistication, he was, in those days.

"We'll finish up later," he said to me, stiffishly. "You'll pick it up all right."

"He doesn't want to pick it up," Fay Muck said, meaning me. "Don't you get that?"

I was for staying, just to cut and thrust with Fay Muck, but for my pal's sake I broke the conference and stood.

The Muck flipped the fluorescent lights on, just to make us blink like hung-over sailors.

"I feel safer already," she said, and left, leaving Larry to shut down.

"It's all right, old man," I said. "You've given me enough to go on."

***

It was well that Larry's magic was so terrible, else I should grow too fond of it. At three o'clock I sat before the formerly foreign contraption, email addresses of Hoepplewhite and Deborah beside me, and typed in the "Larry Berkowitz" subject line: *Viagra $1 a Pop!*

THE CHESTERFIELD HOURS

I dropped my hands into my lap. Let's hold that one in reserve, I thought. I also had a "Jeanine" account set up by Larry, and went to it. In that subject line I entered *Spinning Anyone???*

Ben, I typed,

> *Hi!!! Cant beleive im doing this but honest its about business well mostly anyway!! When u gonna join spinning its the best esp. for you're thighs and butt tho I bet u don't get to many complants!! They really get on our case to sign up new members its not just working out and "lookin good" you have to SELL!!! For spinning I will give u a free month thats a $30 value and if u dont luv it my bad u can give me a spankin!!! OK sales pitch over Ben I really want u to "spin me" all I ever do is work and take care of my parents!!! I am a good girl who wants to go bad but only with a guy I already know and respect so much!!! Come workout after dinner Wed. thats when I close the place we can do what u like I cant comitt cuz of my parents lets just get bizzy!!!!!*

>

C u then, J
>

> *ps this is from my home computer the gym let me take some emails and work from home!!*

Fumbling with the mouse – the infernal contraption is NOT a good old Smith-Corona -- I hit Send.

THE CHESTERFIELD HOURS

THE NEW TROJAN HORSE

That was Monday. The fugitives could only have been on a weekender. How could she chance more with the shotten bugger, having only fooled with him at most in cars and coffeehouses? They had gotten a nasty itch and went off to scratch it. But they'd be back now. How had it gone? Where was Deborah?

When I got home I saw that she'd been there. Of course she'd need undies and wardrobe generally. The tiny changes in the house were unsettling: I noticed a scrap of new food in Daisy's dish. The dog came to me, and I took her out back in the yard, where she stayed beside me as a corgi will do, steady-working and loyal.

"What can you tell me, dear Daisy?" I said.

Of course you cannot locate people today. They don't sit home and when they return don't answer the telephone. For every age, though, there is a Trojan Horse. It seems but a fortnight since the events I describe, and already they're on to texting and tweeting. But in the Two-Thousand Oughts the dodgiest people always, from anywhere, would open the electronic mail with trust and anticipation. So long as it offered pleasure without cost, they could not leave it alone…

Once inside again, gingerly I switched on Deborah's computer. This time I went to my very own new address, set up by Larry in case I wanted it (I hadn't).

THE CHESTERFIELD HOURS

I composed various messages to Deborah. Always I aborted them and began again. Deborah's physical irregularities were few, and dear to me. Her tastes were less atrocious than the contemporary norm. Her work did not offend God or nature. Whose did, then?

Instead I pulled out Hoepplewhite's card again. In the subject line I wrote, *Keen to refi.*

In the body I wrote:

Hoepplewhite,

Thanks for your patience, old boy. Am ready to do that deal you'd been "pitching." Realize I'm like every impossible customer: dawdling, procrastinating, etc., then all of a sudden downright hotfoot to get it done. But trust you can accommodate. Do ring ASAP as can't wait. Best, Chesterfield

A hazard of new fortunes, you blighter, I thought as I hit Send.

THE CHESTERFIELD HOURS

THE BOUNDER TAKES THE BAIT

Wednesday, the day of "Jeanine's" invitation to rendevouz, arrived with no reply from Hoepplewhite. Nor had Deborah been back in the house. Nor had she left word. I wished for signs of trouble in paradise. Hoepplewhite was cheap. I remembered that now. Not quite the ticket with a girl fixed on fortune...

I spent a restless dinner hour, eating little, walking Daisy. It was full dark when I pulled into the R & S parking lot at 8:30. I sat fifty yards from the door, behind the wheel with lights off, and waited. Squinting at the illuminated lobby and front desk, I saw Jeanine.

A sport utility vehicle pulled up near the door. I knew, without seeing, the vanity plate: LOCK IN. Hoepplewhite had reddish blonde hair and an unsightly bunching of muscle between his neck and shoulder blades. The gymnasium, ultimately, is a deforming place...

Hoepplewhite climbed out of the SUV, wearing an overcoat over a suit. He had not come to spin, at least in the R & S sense. As the door opened, I saw Jeanine's blonde head turn toward it.

I viewed this with an icy hilarity. Deborah cheating on me was something to discreetly handle in-house. But for this bounder then to cheat on my wife... well, not to say I'd have him nine years a-killing, quite. But to do my duty would feel like holiday...

THE CHESTERFIELD HOURS

THE WORLD SET TO ROARING

Name of Sender: "Larry Berkowitz"

Subject line: *Viagra $1 a Pop!*

No, scratch that. It had tickled me for a while after Deborah got on about pop-overs, er, pop-ups, er, spam, er… blast the whole pantryful of nauseating glop! Larry said anyway that no one with a brain ever opens them…

Right.

Subject line: *Chesterfield's Blessing*

Message: *Now hear this, Hoepplewhite. Rest assured that no stretch of Caribbean sand, no reserve of Lafit '61, no exertions of your grotesque and hoggish physique can effect the transfer of Deborah's affections to a scullion like yourself. You guppy.*

ps – Recently with my early warning radar blaring it amused me to tell D. you had millions. So better cut a splash – you wouldn't want to disappoint in yet another department.

Might some third party happen upon this loaded missive? Oh, right – Deborah might. I'd take it as a bonus, were she to see it and so tear out his whiskers that he'd think twice in future.

Yet I felt not clever at all. Head in my hands, you know. Bollocks this sterile cyber world, I longed for the physical settlement: a dagger, say, into the goon's disgusting hump. People were not even alive today. Had they forgotten that our blood must be set to running? If not spilled, at least it must move within…

There was a bump downstairs as I clumsily finished shutting down. I descended. Daisy was running to the door.

Deborah stood in the hallway. She looked up at me as I stood motionless on the stairs, and she bent and felt for Daisy who leaned against her. The front door remained ajar.

Which way she would break, I hadn't the slightest. A bolting wife so disorders a house that her return seems to set the world to roaring. Yet no one spoke.

She squatted now as she pulled Daisy to her. She wore no coat, she belonged neither here nor there…

I took another step down, and another. Deborah stood and seemed actually to waver before me. Surely Hoepplewhite called to her, with pretty lies…

Yet for myself, I felt clean again. A gentleman does not Send to his wife -- he speaks to her.

"There is no Fortune," I said to Deborah. Would she stay or would she go?

Daisy, unnerved, piddled on the carpet at the feet of Deborah, who stood anchored there.

"You lie," she said.

"I have a mistress," I said – lobbing another one, what? "She's upstairs just now."

"You're a sixth grade teacher," she said, "with barely a dog." Daisy, shame-faced, dragged her bum circularly over the carpet, snuffled, then streaked out the open door.

"Of course you realize," I said, "that Hoepplewhite's been buggering after *me* for years. 'Leave her,' he says, 'leave the doxy and be with me.' Quite pathetic."

"So are you," she said. "Doxy is *your* word. Or is it the eighteenth century's?"

Finally I stepped down and faced her straight on. Daisy's pee stain settled between us like a sodden chaperone.

"If he's out there a-waiting on you," I said, "Daisy's after killing him."

"He's not," she said. Her long auburn hair was tousled, her eye make-up slightly off, her cheeks reddish with winter. "And he couldn't be more dead to me already."

I heard the dog barking, far off and going away.

"Well," I said, "I'd better fetch her."

I stepped out of the glaring hall and into the night. Daisy dashed willy-nilly through the backyard of the house across the street, yelping like a dingo.

I heard Deborah throw the lock behind me. A rummy sound, that, not much like make-up foreplay.

I might have seen it coming. To pee and flee – Daisy, I mean, not Deborah – meant my valiant pooch still smelt turpitude like a dead rat in the basement.

But a gentleman with a wife, any wife, has a duty to her. And my guv'nor says a guy who freezes in no-man's land soon gets frozen stiff.

"Take heart, Daisy," I called, pushing on. "We all are halfway home now."

I crossed over the street.   END BOOK ONE, PART ONE

Part Two

CHESTERFIELD GETS DOWN

"Are you down yet?"

I looked up from my grading book. Arlene Grimmboat, a third grade teacher who normally spent lunch hour at needlepoint, stared at me like a hen eyeing a grub.

"Beg pardon?" I said. "I didn't catch."

Arlene turned to Suzette Borch and snorted "Hel-*lo*? Eagles goin' to the Super Bowl!" She uttered this last as a kind of tribal chant.

"Like he'd have a clue," said Suzette. She was "Missy Borch" to her second graders, "Blow Torch" to us male colleagues.

"Sorry," I told Grimmboat. "I guess I'm not myself." And neither are you, Grime Bat, I thought, or you'd be a-knitting.

"He misses his wife," said Carrie Hahn, a young kindergarten teacher with an unnerving sentimental streak.

"Ah," I said, ignoring her and addressing Grime Bat. "If the question is whether I have a wager on the game, the answer is no. I am not down."

"How did I guess?" said Blow Torch. "Like he'd know from football."

"Certainly, though," I said, "a betting man would have to take the Eagles. Seven points is too generous a spread to pass up."

This elicited grudging approval. "The Eagles won't win," I added, "but they'll assuredly cover."

"What?!"

"You f---ing traitor!"

Larry Berkowitz, technology director and my only nearby male colleague, entered the lounge and sat on my other flank.

"Jesus," he muttered. "What are you stirring up the yentas for?"

"It's extraordinary," I said, "how mad the town's gone in only two weeks."

"Well, it's been twenty-four years," Larry said, meaning for the Eagles. "But don't tell me that's what *these* broads are screeching about?"

"Twenty-four years since what?" Blow Torch said. "Since you got laid?"

Grime Bat guffawed. Carrie Hahn turned away blushing.

Male minority always found out Larry more painfully than it did me, who at least had been loved before left.

"It *is* the Super Bowl they're on about," I said directly to Larry, as if the women were mere detention rowdies. "And if it's got into *them,* what's to stop it turning Philadelphia into bloody Jonestown?"

At which point Carrie Hahn related an anecdote disturbing yet useful...

THANK YOU, YOUNG CARRIE

"Like he'd have a clue about football."

But Blow Torch had misjudged the Book of Chesterfield, having never read past the jacket copy of my diction and manners. From birth I'd imbibed the legend of the '60 Eagles, of Van Brocklin, Bednarik and Retzlaff, who repulsed the mighty Packers in a pale and crystalline December sunlight. Eternally it seemed to live as Philadelphia's first Technicolor moment, to martial music that sang in the blood...

Yet I was damned if I'd get down now. Don't think, by the way, that a gentleman is automatically a stick and a prude. On the contrary, I occasionally enjoy what my mum calls a sporting flutter. The ponies are more in her line, by the way. But betting on football was disagreeable and bootless. I didn't much like the current Eagles, apart from their quarterback, a cheerful warrior of the good old kind.

"So my friend Marcy's husband took out a second mortgage to bet on the Eagles, and he like forged her signature..."

Carrie Hahn's tale was filtered by the other teachers through their own investment in the Eagles' chances. My vantage lay elsewhere. Here was the kind of sordid calamity a gentleman could properly wish on his worst enemy. Benedict Hoepplewhite, mortgage broker, wife-stealer and cur, was all but overqualified.

"Are you even certain, dear," said my mother Daphne over Sunday brunch, "that Ben and Deborah left you sporting the horns? It all seemed to pass like Bottom's dream."

"Oh, they had their innings, Mother. But hear what I've got for the bugger. Carrie Hahn says -- "

"I mean to say, Deborah seems to have done with all men."

"That never takes," said my father. "Just find her for me and you'll see nature's way."

"Oh, rot, Jack."

"Dad! Mother! Peace!" I clinked a spoon to my juice glass. "No one can get hold of Hoepplewhite or Deborah either one, or I'd have killed him and made her my right wife again, on a bed of Swedish memory foam."

"All right, dear," Daphne said. "So tell us about this nice Carrie girl. Is there something we should know?"

"She's my colleague! She's only twenty-four!"

"Deborah must be thirty-one if she's a day," said Jack, sixty-six as you know. "When can I meet young Carrie?"

I sighed and pushed away from the table. "Thanks for breakfast." The Carrie Hahn mortgage stratagem wanted cold, sexless intelligence…

THE CHESTERFIELD HOURS

THE HAMMER

"Didn't we drop the hammer on this Edelweiss clown already?" Larry Berkowitz said. "The phony emails did the trick, right?" We sat before my pal's master control center in the darkened tech lab.

"It's Hoepplewhite, Benedict Hoepplewhite," I said. "Right, you were brilliant, and they're no longer beasting it with two backs. But there's no statute of limitations for his sort."

"All right then," Larry said, booting up, the good old gleam back in his eyes. "So how do you want to jam the bastard this time?"

The door squealed open, and that sickly hall light again blighted Larry's spell. Fay Muck, our sainted principal, had chivvied us out once more.

"Well well," she said, "another session of Windows for Dummies."

"For Luddites, Ms. Muck," I corrected her. "Kindly apply to me the proper epithet – as I would to you."

Larry cleared his throat and managed to croak, "It's all about the Super Bowl."

Fay Muck stepped toward us and surveyed the screen. Upon her entrance Larry had deftly punched a football link and it came up just in time.

"You're sure, Mister Berkowitz, that it isn't all about hotbabes.com?"

I said, "Really it's all about ruthless technology versus human intuition, Ms. Muck. The Super Bowl being a perfect laboratory, and Larry and I rival theoreticians."

Fay Muck fixed me with a savage look. "What about ruthless humanity?" She then turned to Larry. "What about idiot technology?"

"Elegantly provocative!" I said. "Cats lie with dogs, mere anarchy loosed upon the world. Trust you, Ms. Muck."

"If only it were mutual," our major domo said and walked out the door.

"She kicked her husband out, you know," Larry said. "Gambling and stuff."

"Ah. Well, a gentleman doesn't inquire."

A gentleman might, however, usefully discern patterns. At the junior high and high schools were many male teachers who bet football. Slips were collected, of autumn Fridays, by a city garbageman and nephew of Philadelphia's CEO for the good old Sicilian fraternity. Money flowed, in the way of the world, from the credulous multitudes to the ready few...

" ...took out a second mortgage to bet on the Eagles..."

...and if the teaching brethren, and the hapless Mister Muck, and probably even Grime Bat and Blow Torch were all coming croppers at games, how many equity billions might tumble down the tidy bowl should the Philly proletariat fully extend itself?

"You understand," I said, "our fellow can't get enough of lucre. He's a bloody gluttonous hog, defined by dollars, and that's how we'll have him."

"I wish I was defined by dollars," Larry said.

"Oh no you don't. You have your worries, as we all do, but your passion is the objective truths you wring out of this machine of yours. My passion is imparting to this sixth-grade clay a civilised ethic for a rancid and faithless age."

"If I had the money," Larry said, "then I'd have the women."

I thought of my lovely Deborah, who by rights should have rebounded to my forgiving self after the one inexplicable weekend with Hoepplewhite. Instead she was in a virtual nunnery of solitude, forfeiting our house and gardens, our beloved dog Daisy, our intimacies…

"Old boy," I told Larry, "you're going to see a river of money flow toward friend Hoepplewhite. But his final wages will be nothing you envy."

Larry's brows bunched peevishly. "He should go without women too. That would be justice."

This might have come very near me, but I took it not amiss. I clapped Larry on the shoulder. "I say again, money defines him. If we do our main job, no woman will raise him with derrick or pulley. So lead on, webmaster."

***

We sought, before all else, true believers.

WE DON'T LEND TO PUSSIES.

OUR FUNDS ARE AVAILABLE ONLY TO THOSE WILLING TO BET THE EAGLES TO <u>WIN</u>, NOT COVER!!!

"You don't write like you talk," Larry said.

"Well," I said, "American manhood lingers as I see it somewhere between denial and acceptance on the old Kubler-Ross. You've got to appeal to what they've got left, or wish they had."

41

THE CHESTERFIELD HOURS

All responses, in Larry's ingenius design, would funnel to Hoepplewhite's business email as application requests, stripped of any reference to the game. Hoepplewhite, since the Deborah affair, had gone virtual and invisible.

No worry of mine, you tumor, thought I. Dwell you in cyberspace or in a spider hole, I'll have you all the same.

NEEDLING GRIME BAT

It was Monday, Super Bowl Week. The city, and the nation, obsessed on the status of an injured and temperamental Eagles wide receiver. Could he, would he go on Sunday?

"I don't care," said Grime Bat over lunch. She was back to knitting, but barbarously, her needles stabbing the poor yarn as if it were a Cowboys jersey. "My bet is down and that's that. You gotta have faith."

"But can this war be won?" I said -- just innocently chaffing the old girl, what?

Grime Bat upshot one needle through her baby grandson's future sweater, and I could feel Larry flinch at my side. "You're a snide sonofabitch," she said.

But sheep were many, and wooly, and bound for the shearing, this week in Philly. I walked with Larry back to pick up my class at the cafeteria.

"Have you got a pulse on the Hoepplewhite thing?"

Larry's eyes bugged. "It's blowing up. The site has crashed at least a couple times."

"Super. He's likely intoxicated with inheriting heaven and earth."

A roar issued from the cafeteria as we reached the big doors. A surly Dylan Czarnecki shrugged off a female aide escorting him from his latest outrage. In their wake was a wailing kindergartener.

"Must go," I told Larry. Why did Principal Muck persist in scheduling my sixth-grade beasts to grub with five-year-olds?

"Listen," Larry called after. "Are you at all worried that we might be putting money in this guy's pockets?"

I was closing on young Dylan. "Not in the slightest," I called back to Larry. The Eagles would cover, but they'd assuredly lose.

THE CHESTERFIELD HOURS

HEAVEN-SENT CARRIE HAHN

The hulking Dylan Czarnecki, rising five feet and a half and tipping one-forty, raged, "I didn't do nothin'!"

"Except wreck the Queen's English and torment the weak," I said. "For which crimes I am the absolute hanging judge."

Twenty feet away Carrie Hahn comforted her sobbing charge, a tiny girl. Dylan almost – almost – deserved immediate off-loading to his mother, an unbalanced harpy given to slapping. We must, I reluctantly decided, consider what's best for everyone. But what in the nation would that be?

As with the mortgage refi scheme, Carrie Hahn providentially answered.

Petite, dwarfed even by this sixth-grade Visigoth, she approached with the little girl hugging timorously to her side. "Dylan," she said, "is there something you want to say?"

Czarnecki looked pole-axed. "I'm sorry," he said. He never looked at the kindergartener.

"'I'm sorry, Katarina,'" Carrie coached. "'I'll never do it again.'"

Katarina didn't exist for this remorseless thug, but he mouthed, "I'm sorry, Katarina. I'll never do it again." Dylan's gaze never moved off Carrie Hahn's face.

Good God, I thought. The little warthog's in love!

"That's better." Carrie turned to me. "What did they expect, putting your big kids with my little punkins?"

My junior colleague did have deucedly distracting green eyes. But duty comes first and always.

"It's housecats with tigers," I told her – crisply, you know. "I'll speak to Muck about it."

Dylan, sweating, with an orange stain ringing his mouth, stood stupidly mooning at Carrie Hahn. I am keener to punish this lout, I admitted to myself, than I am to improve him. Yet I am charged to do both. I bent to pat little Katarina, who held to Carrie's leg like a koala bear to a tree.

"I'm bound to say, Miss Hahn," I said, "that a rote apology hardly seems to have made full amends to our Katarina, or to you, or to myself."

Those green eyes caught my implication and leapt beyond. Carrie turned back to the miscreant.

"Dylan," she said, "this must never happen again, and I would like to see you learn to protect the little ones instead of hurting them. Since you've given Mr. Chesterfield no choice but to revoke some of your recess time, I'm going to suggest that you spend that time doing jobs for me in my room. Mr. Chesterfield?"

Dylan, nodding dumbly, was already gone over to her.

She *was* an angel from Provvy! "Let's make it a month!" I said hilariously. The long, claustrophobic late winter of indoor recess, of Dylan and his B.O., his sadism toward girls and his dampening effect on class spirit, was spanned in a trice. What a girl…

BETTER GET BRACED

Days and nights at home, there was no denying, were hard now. Modest as our Cape abode was, it bulked cavernous and hollow with Deborah a month gone. I had, I liked to think, inner resources. I ran with Daisy morning and night, and spoke to and stroked her as I read on the sofa of nights. I saw my parents betimes, but not overmuch. On Super Bowl Thursday I even gave a cocktail hour for fellow teachers, at which Carrie Hahn insisted on helping to serve and do dishes. Larry drank two beers and fell asleep. The party anticipated what in effect was a nationwide long weekend and it went pretty well…

At nine o'clock my mother called.

"My dear," she said, "Granny Victoria is very poorly. We'd better get braced, I'm afraid."

This required bracing indeed, though no one was readier for her to shuffle off the coil than Granny V herself, at ninety-one. No, the true awful weight of anticipation centered on The Fortune, which came down through my mother's people, the Ffoulkes, like a cruel generational joke.

"How sad, Mother," I said, "for all of us, and you above all."

"Righto. Look, dear, your father's bellowing something at me. So there you have it, and you know I'll level with you when the time comes." She rang off.

So there it was. Daphne and Jack, and I after them, were to accept our three-score and ten of genteel poverty, of smallish houses and frugal holidays. The Fortune – if it were even real – amounted to a sort of afterlife.

With this thought, in the aftermath of my little party, I came back to myself. I looked about for Daisy. Yes, no denying days and nights at home were hard now. I wasn't even bothered that some might consider it was Deborah off playing the man: staying in dives, furtively coming round for this and that, bolting again before conversation went past niceties. And rumoured to be... God help us... speed-dating...

"Hello?"

Her voice found me changing upstairs. Of the cocktail party there was now no trace, thanks to young Carrie, and somewhat to Larry. The spotless house would doubtless annoy Deborah...

"You up there? Where's Daisy?"

Of course she had her own key. No gentleman would quibble at that. He, and the house, are at the wife's disposal...

Daisy was running to her. This, as always on these stealth visits, brought from Deborah a surge of feeling.

"You Daisy! You good girl!"

"Missing you," I said matter-of-factly from atop the stairs. I omitted the pronoun and helping verb, so that the subject in fact could be Daisy. I needed to compose myself.

Daisy capered around the legs of my wife, who bent to stroke her. Deborah wore, against the mid-winter winds that had been so vicious, a long camel coat. She was hatless, red-faced, and her long brown hair was everywhere: inside her lapels, splashed down her back, in her face.

She also held an object immediately familiar, yet wrong somehow on her own person. "Whose scarf is this?"

"Ah," I said, in recognition. "Young Carrie. Forget her head next. I'll take it in to school tomorrow."

"Young Carrie?" Deborah, on these nocturnal pop-ins, would enter with an attitude both guilty and pugnacious and then, finding me as always alone with Daisy, soften like caramel. And then bolt again, to leave me shaking. Now with the paisley scarf draped over her camel sleeve she assumed a nauseous rigidity.

Something impelled me for once not to hang back, but rather to descend the stairs to meet her. I drew the scarf from Deborah and at the same time kissed her on the cheek, not perfunctorily but amorously, sliding my lips subtly toward the neck below her ear. I mean, it wasn't hard work.

"I threw a small Thursday for the faculty, pretty well-attended actually. Cheerful-like, did me some good, I think -- "

"Get your face off me," she snarled, shoving me back. "Who the f--- is Carrie?"

"Steady on, dear. That's not your lingo, nor was ever your style."

Again not waiting on her, not waiting for the pop-in to rotten, I turned back to climb the stairs. I heard Deborah take breath.

"Who -- "

"Teaches kindergarten, you know," I said over my shoulder. "One of the bunch." I was climbing, she was in my wake.

Astonishing, I thought. Her every pop-in till now had left me morose and desolate: the powerlessness and futility; Deborah's pats for me and Daisy; her abrupt dismissal of us both and her exit. Desolating. But now...what was this welling of uplift I felt, this sense that I was literally rising?

"Good night, dear. Daisy misses -- "

But Daisy, leaving Deborah, rocketed past me and beat me to the top of the stairs.

Carrie Carrie Moon Child, I thought, laying the scarf over my doorknob. Three times now you've been the charm.

THE CHESTERFIELD HOURS

DOMINIC, AND CARRIE'S FIVE LITTLE TINY ONES

My suspicion that The Fortune, real or not, was a curse had deepened with the Hoepplewhite/Deborah affair. My noble but inebriated mother had put The Fortune in Deborah's mind, causing her to wish it into our hands ahead of its excruciating schedule. Still, six years passed that were otherwise happy. Then gone she was, gone off with a Hoepplewhite obscenely enriched on buckets of refi dollars, a classic mistaking of brains for a bull market.

All very painful, notwithstanding a break-up after one weekend that spoke of something fantastically repellent in friend Hoepplewhite. Who, what was this Hoepplewhite?

I wasn't sure I anymore cared, since the Night of the Scarf. Deborah's refusal to rejoin me on the good old path had baffled and saddened me, till that night. Then with the angel's weight of Carrie's scarf on my arm, my climb with Daisy up the stairs and away from Deborah, I had, in a spontaneous and unwilled way, let her go. Funny...

And Hoepplewhite? Habitual greed, a fitfully attentive Almighty, and the inexorable swings of capital markets would settle accounts one day.

It was with a renewed sense of balance that I left the house on Super Bowl Friday. The Eagles' injured and self-dramatizing wide receiver would play on Sunday. Hobbled or not, this prima donkey would command defensive attention, and thus help the Eagles to cover, though they'd assuredly lose.

There was commotion in the custodial area as I entered school that Friday. This was also the place where smokers smoked, gossips gossiped, and decorum fell away generally. I spied Grime Bat and Blow Torch among others, and Carrie Hahn. In the center of the group was an outsider, a little dark-haired man in a bulging black goose-down coat with enormous work gloves sticking out of one pocket. He held papers of different sizes in each hand, and a pen. As I approached, the man regarded me with a mix of suspicion and good humor.

"Good morning, Mr. Chesterfield," Carrie said with a warm colorization of the practiced in-school formality (though no children were in evidence). "This is Dominic."

I extended my hand to the man's which was already in motion. "How are you, sir?" I said.

The little man now smiled and looked me guilelessly in the eyes as we shook. "Pleased to meetcha." Here too, Carrie Hahn had softened the way with a word.

"Dominic just stopped by to take any last Super Bowl bets," Carrie said. "He's still giving seven."

"Like he'd have a clue," Blow Torch muttered, meaning of course me. The awestruck way she and Grime Bat regarded Dominic suggested that *he* held clues to the Super Bowl, to cold fusion, to the hereafter.

I held back. I was not, these past few days, unhappy. I no longer missed Deborah. Of course Hoepplewhite still rated thumbscrews, Drano enemas, al Quaeda death squads. But – only this nagged at me – what innocent persons, known and unknown, might sit like ducks in the line of fire?

"You can put me down for five, Dom," Carrie said.

I blinked and came back to myself. *Dom*, she called him!

"You mean five large?" Dominic said, clearly charmed and pulling the girl's leg.

"As if!" Carrie said, pushing on the little man's puffy black sleeve. "Five little tiny ones."

Was there not goodness here, something very dear? Five! I was thinking how for several years I'd taken Deborah every Friday night to a friendly neighborhood Italian bistro we both enjoyed. In the time she'd been gone I'd saved perhaps three hundred I would have spent...

"If it's seven you're giving, Dom," I said, "put me down for a hundred."

"I don't f---ing believe it," Grime Bat said. She turned to Dominic. "I put fifty down already on the Eagles before you came here. Put me down for fifty more, to win, and next season don't be a stranger."

Dominic, polite, good-humoured, earnest, seemed like any other good merchant who puts service first.

"My bad," he said. "I figured yez are all women and being busy I let this building slide." He nodded and smiled at me, then turned back to Grime Bat and said, "I'd be very innerested to know who you put the first fifty down with."

At this, I took my leave. As I rounded the corner toward my classroom Carrie was whispering something to Dominic.

LA MUCK CHUCKS OUT LE

With my class off at gym I took the chance to see Principal Muck about the lunchroom situation. Friendly as I was now with young Carrie, neither of us liked our two classes eating together. If I could have a word...

"F--- you!"

"No, f--- *you*!"

A shadow fled across the illuminated window that said:

Dr. Fay Muck

Building Principal

The door opened and another strange man stepped out. Blinking, red-nosed but with ashen jowls, he looked like he'd rolled here from tavern closing time, via the gutter. Thinning hair askew, he blinked again at me, who stood frozen as if beholding some nightmare double.

"My name is Muck," the man said.

"Of course," I said.

"We've got some things to sort out," the man said, cocking his head to the closed door.

"Ah." I studied this poor wretch, thought of Fay Muck, and imagined a resident of Dresden sorting it out with the RAF. The lunchroom issue could wait...

"So who do you like in the game?" the man said.

Easing away, I was. "Well, the Eagles should certainly cover."

"I've got 'em to win," Muck said. "It's all coming together now."

"All luck to you," I said, fleeing. "In everything."

THE CHESTERFIELD HOURS

THE GOOD OLD ANGLICAN MERCY

Granny Victoria was rallying yet again. This was happiness to me, as I loved my grandmother and regarded The Fortune increasingly with distaste and foreboding. Mother Daphne, the would-be heiress, seemed unmoved and incurious, while father Jack soldiered on with his wife, his pension, and his fond reflections on old conquests, military and other.

Far removed as I stood already from The Fortune, I consciously put it even further. Daphne's mere boozy mention to Deborah had let in the Hoepplewhite incubus six years later. And lust for Fortune, I'd seen just recently, only served to enslave the pitiable Mister Mucks of the world. The bloody human toll…

" …*took out a second mortgage to bet on the Eagles…* "

Right. It's not the Hoepplewhites who need thinking of…

" …*and he like forged her signature.*"

…it's the poor sods who mean well and can't help themselves, even including, I decided in a burst of charity, the Blow Torches and Grime Bats, who are always with us.

And I, bent on gutting Hoepplewhite, had trifled with those sods who, if they could be saved by no one but themselves, at least didn't need being fed matches in the dynamite factories of their own tortured psyches.

At lunchtime I sought out Larry. Grime Bat and Blow Torch were emboldened after doubling down that morning. As I entered the lounge

Grime Bat called out, "Here's Braveheart himself. I guess you'll win about ten bucks on your hundred dollars *to cover*."

I allowed myself a small smile. "May we all reap as we have sown."

I put a hand on the shoulder of Larry, who sat eating microwaved macaroni and cheese.

"We're to the tech lab," I said. "You don't want to eat that anyway."

***

ALL BETS ON THE EAGLES TO WIN SHOULD BE TAKEN OFF NOW!!!

WE KNOW SOMETHING YOU DON'T.

TO TAKE YOUR BET OFF, GO TO THE LINK BELOW AND CLICK "CANCEL APP."

"I never know whether we're hurting this guy or helping him," Larry said as he put the finishing touches on.

"I confess I'm not certain myself. But I'm thinking not of him, but of the poor chumps." Hoepplewhite was passing from my concern, my consciousness, my life. At least I hoped so.

"But," Larry said, "the chumps are going to be chumps no matter what. This guy Hoepplewhite really did you, and just as your friend I'd like to break his legs with a sledge hammer. I'd like to smash his nose back into his brain."

"Not, since Masada, a recourse characteristic of your excellent tribe," I said. "But it makes a pretty picture."

Larry had his arrow on the Send button. "Well then," he said, "are we done here?"

There was no knowing how Larry's design might have shaken the earth. The Eagles would assuredly cover yet lose. The chumps would have lost hearth, home, and Marcy. Hoepplewhite would first be picking through a billion dollars in loans gone bad, then once we leaked his identity would have looked up to see the chumps advancing on him like Robespierre's minions. It had had, as the football coaches say, potential.

"We're done, old man," I told Larry. "Send it on."

For all the awesome power of my pal's webwork, I felt the matter had come right in the end. I wished for Deborah and Hoepplewhite, if not the plunder they craved, at least no harm. And most importantly I sensed approval by the good old Anglican deity who made dogs and trout streams, has humour, and stands like a Gentleman mostly out of the way.

MERCY WITHDRAWN

Public school teachers, unbeknownst to the larger public, are among its earliest risers. An 8:15 school day means you are in the building by 7:45. Civilising preparations – washing, tea or coffee, proper dress and grooming – take their own good time. Add a daily three-mile dog run and you are necessarily up with the lark.

For me this iron regimen did not go away on weekends. *Sans* alarm clock I awoke by six, generally with Daisy on the bed and licking my face. Super Bowl Saturday went by the script.

For the bone-chilling dawn I donned gym shorts and tee, topped the tee with cotton jersey, sweatshirt and finally windbreaker, and put lined nylon running pants over the shorts. Daisy got a wool body sweater and booties, and betimes I'd rub up her nose and ears.

For the game next day I was having over Carrie and Larry, neither of whom had nearby family, and who shared with me a mercenary interest in the result. This morning I wanted to pick up two loaves from an ancient Italian bakery where you could buy bread hot from the oven. The bakery being closed Sundays, I would take one loaf home to devour immediately with eggs, and freeze the other for my Super Bowl offering.

Daisy and I trotted and puffed along the good old streets. Man and dog blew plumes of steam as we approached the bakery. It was housed in a ramshackle building near a strip mall whose tenants included Ripped &

Shredded, the gymnasium where Deborah and Hoepplewhite had been members.

A strange sight there brought us up short. A blocky figure with hair of copper wire stepped out of the gym, bundled in goose down and carrying a large bag. Hoepplewhite, a natural fatso unnaturally preoccupied with arm and shoulder exercises, had built slabs of bunchy muscle onto his upper torso, which with his reddish hair made him into a sort of human gila monster. Here, in the grudging dawn, he was out from under his rock.

I saw on the street the SUV with the vanity plate LOCK IN, and as casually as possible cut the owner off there.

"Well, Hoepplewhite."

The gila monster's eyes flared for a moment with fear, then assumed their normal lifelessness.

"Chesterfield."

"How's business?"

Hoepplewhite temporized by opening the truck door and throwing in his bag. Then he put on a triumphalist smile.

"It just gets better and better. If it all ended today I could retire."

"A big frantic push to lock in before rates rise?" I said – provocatively, you know.

Hoepplewhite studied me. He seemed to have got his footing again, which I rather resented.

"Oh sure. But you wouldn't know anything about that, would you? You finally learned to use a computer the past couple months, huh?"

I snuck a wee glance toward the gym reception desk…

"Aha! You're busted, pal!" Hoepplewhite crowed. "I saw you looking for Jeanine just now. I knew it was you all the time."

I felt myself go white. "Sorry?" Daisy was growling at Hoepplewhite.

"Don't play dumb. Just for your information, I went ahead and banged her anyway. So thanks, pal. I'm outta here."

As he climbed into the SUV, I caught the door. Daisy lunged at Hoepplewhite's ankle as it swung into the truck.

"You parasitic hyena," I said. "I challenge you to a duel tomorrow at noon, on the site of the late demolished Veterans Stadium."

"Are you nuts?" Hoepplewhite said, his eyes wide.

"Firearms within city limits are naturally out of the question," I said. "We will duel with axes."

"With *what*?" Hoepplewhite, with his free hand, turned the ignition.

"Doubtless you have no axe," I said, "but I have two. You just be there at noon, and bring a second."

Only the SUV itself had the strength to break my hold on the door, and Hoepplewhite used it by flooring the gas pedal and ripping away.

I stood with Daisy in the lurch, feeling soiled and shamed. Jeanine, forgive me, I thought.

ATONE AND GET COOKING

"Will you come with us to visit Granny today, dear?" mother Daphne said, while serving up my eggs and bangers. It was nine a.m. on Super Sunday.

"Actually, Mother, I popped in on her late yesterday, because I'm quite booked today. I'm fighting a duel at noon and then I've got to run home and cook for my Super Bowl guests."

"Well, that was very sweet of you. But you never allow yourself time enough, you cram things in so."

"I don't want any phone calls or any interruptions whatsoever from two p.m. to midnight," father Jack said. "I'll be in the den with the doors closed."

"Dad, don't waste time on that pre-game rubbish. Kick-off's at 6:18. Read your book, take a walk."

Captain Jack sipped his coffee and looked absently out into his tiny, frozen yard. "I suppose I could check out this duel of yours. Where is it?"

"It's all the way out at the Vet," I said.

"You're not getting out of visiting my mother!" Daphne said.

"All right, all right."

Of course the old guv'nor didn't miss much. Leaving Daisy at home, I arrived at the desolate Vet site ten minutes early. At 12:30 I packed my axes back into the car and left. The craven gila monster was back under his rock. What did a default victory do for either justice or Jeanine?

THE CHESTERFIELD HOURS

Certainly the Creator would approve the severance of Hoepplewhite's picnic-ham neck, but He knew just as surely that His good soldier – yours truly -- had lately played the pimp with a gullible, if dyed and inked, maiden.

Once I'd returned home and put away the axes, I paced the foyer. Daisy, stirring from sleep, joined me. Perhaps Jeanine had been, like all the chumps, only too ready and willing to play with fire; perhaps we make our own beds; perhaps…

Perhaps bollocks. With Jeanine unatoned for, calling the bowsers off Hoepplewhite on Friday had been a sham gesture, and Provvy summarily dished me for it on Saturday, showing me a nemesis gloatingly unscathed and unapologetic.

I pulled Daisy to me and knelt at the bottom of the good old staircase. Dispensing with puerile promises to attend this or that many church services, rejecting utterly any mercy toward Hoepplewhite, I asked simply forgiveness for Jeanine.

"Right," I said, rising again, and I went and got cooking for my friends.

THE CHESTERFIELD HOURS

GAME'S UP, HOEPPLEWHITE

The expected spiritual lift went missing as the Eagles, after drawing first blood, fell into sandlot bungling. The quarterback, my favorite, kept chucking the ball toward the wrong jerseys. The egocentric wide receiver was the only Philly standout. During time-outs, a pampered young heiress, insensible to her generational peers on distant battlefields, vamped and preened in hamburger commercials. Not speaking of a superbly professional New England team, the wrong people were everywhere winning out.

With two minutes to play the Eagles trailed by ten. The game – The Game, in its larger sense – was up.

I recognized my sin with Jeanine had been a large one. Provvy, however beneficent, is not one's Pal, and not to be so taken for granted. When you play human pawns, toward whatever cause, you're throwing in with every Hoepplewhite who acts the locust with decent lives. Atonement for this would take time and, apparently, a sore lesson.

At the two-minute warning I wobbled to my feet, picked up my guests' dirty dishes and took them to the sink. I'd prepared chicken and spinach lasagna, and set out a gargantuan bottle of chianti, a year-old gift which so embarrassed Deborah that she wouldn't serve it, and from whose casing could be built a bamboo palace. Larry, Carrie and I had drunk the bulk of it, and as the Eagles circled the drain, the plonk we'd tossed back seemed to depress rather than elate us.

"You bums," Larry scolded to the TV. "Those Eagles-to-win schmucks deserve what they get, but why do us smart guys have to lose money on this?"

"Because we're not smart after all." The game was already far from me. Hoepplewhite remained near. I scraped lasagna remnants into the garbage. My creation, so appetizing when I was hungry, now faintly disgusted me. But then, I was disgusted with my very self.

Carrie Hahn was at my elbow. She couldn't not be helpful. She wore a flattering, body-hugging turtleneck and Hepburnesque flannel slacks. Her brown hair was cut short and pixieish, and her oval face was dominated by those big ingenuous green eyes.

"Shall I cork the wine?" she said.

"Not if you want more."

"Oh no. You?"

"No, I'm pipped," I said, and looked into those green eyes. "I'm sorry you're losing your fiver."

She smiled. "Haven't lost it yet. There's *always* hope!"

One can't trifle with such innocence. Sure, I wanted to kiss her just that moment. But I, a josser of thirty-two, would eat my liver before touching this sweet child. A woman amongst men often wants and revels in a different kind of talk, a different kind of friend. It can work wonderfully both ways, but bloody men will bung it up every time...

Not this lad, thought I.

Another commercial came on, as I and Carrie finished loading the dishwasher. How *would* they ever finish this game? A forty-minute halftime, a bombardment of programming promos... four and a half hours now...

"I want to thank you guys," Carrie said when we were seated again, "for not mentioning that Hoepplewhite all evening. Talk about a bum!"

"Come again?" I felt a tectonic jolt, plates from different strata scraping on one another. What was Hoepplewhite to *her*?

"Oh God," Carrie said, "Larry's so mad you let that guy off the hook after what he did to you."

"Oh," I said. "*Is* Larry?"

Larry slumped dejectedly in his chair. The hangdog Eagles broke the huddle. Larry, eyes fixed on the screen, waved a hand in the air. "Context," he said to Carrie. "Context, please."

"Right, Larry," I gritted. "What's the context, old boy?"

"Let her tell you," Larry said.

"Well," Carrie said, "Larry says you could have ruined the guy but you didn't because you're a gentleman of the old school. And he's mad but I think it's just the best to know a man whose mercy is not strained!"

God, she was a stellar girl, but Hoepplewhite breathing free air blighted everything.

Larry, his chin on his chest, said, "You shouldn't *let* people like that off the hook."

No, you shouldn't... but if a villain won't come out to be killed...

The Eagles ran a play to nowhere as the clock ticked down. They would assuredly lose *and* fail to cover.

"Well," young Carrie said, "fear not. Dominic's on the case."

"Sorry?" With a minute and a half to play, I was off in a funk.

Daisy, who had been resting on the rug, stretched then climbed into the lap of Carrie, who stroked her long ears.

Carrie said, "You know how Dom was so curious to know who else was taking football action, like for Arlene and Suzette?"

"Yes?"

"Well, I'm like, who's taking more action than this bum Hoepplewhite? So I told Dom."

Oh rare, I thought. "And Dom replied?"

The girl made a winsome face and stroked Daisy, who lay blissed out in her arms.

"He's such a dear. He said he's buried all weekend with family stuff, church, his kid's hockey game, a Super Bowl party. But he said he'd get on it first thing Monday, and he thanked me very much."

At that, the Eagles' cheerful warrior quarterback threw over the top not to the diva star receiver, but to a young unknown, for a touchdown. The extra point brought the deficit to three. The Eagles had covered. *Contra* Grime Bat's jeer, I had quadrupled my hundred, Carrie her five.

Larry leapt from his chair, bellowed *"Oofah!"* and rent the air with his fist.

"Oh yay!" said young Carrie, still with Daisy in her lap.

Larry pointed to Carrie and said, "Tell Dom that's Hoepplewhite with an 'o.' *Benedict* Hoepplewhite."

Provvy, I thought. I reached across and took young Carrie's hand. "Will you be my pal?" I said.

"I am your pal," she said.

Daisy licked our joined hands. Small "p" of course, I thought. Right.

END BOOK ONE, PART TWO

Part Three

CHESTERFIELD GETS A DATE

A bolting wife disorders a house.

This truth had lodged in my mind some weeks before, with Deborah dislodged by her own impulse from our Cape Cod. The house in her absence had gone quiet, yet in its essence, unquiet. When Deborah slipped back in one night, after a failed weekender with the villain Hoepplewhite, I from the top of the stairs had locked gazes with her. For an eternity, no word was spoken… yet all the world roared in my ears. Our dog Daisy ran deranged circles round Deborah, piddled at her feet, and shot out the open front door.

Dogs left their dens and went distantly barking. The woman slipped back out into a scarlet-black night. That had been disorder.

For order there was school, where I taught sixth grade between iron bells of eight and three of the clock. 7:45: walk in, settle, and greet the good old colleagues. 8:00: lay the lessons out and mark the board. 8:15: call the students to order and take attendance. Then Reading, next Math, next the day's Special, next Lunch…

Right. For order, there was school…

THE CHESTERFIELD HOURS

"Mr. Chesterfield, your wife's here. I'm sending her down." Click.

I replaced the faculty room phone. The first eyes mine met were those of Grime Bat Grimmboat, third grade teacher and pitiless matron. Not the girl to share with...

"Jesus, who died?" said Larry Berkowitz.

I turned to my pal. "Deborah's in the building."

"Here?" Larry's panic, and my own sense that my face had combusted, spoke to something –

"Hi! Am I interrupting anything?"

Deborah of course looked smashing. It was late winter and her complexion betrayed no weather cracking. Her lush auburn hair welled up from her coat collar and her brown eyes were bright and lovely.

I stood. I could sense Berkowitz goggling behind me, as if Aeon Flux, say, had stepped out Larry's nearest erotic realm.

"Well, dear," I said, taking Deborah's hands in mine. "Welcome to the fetid bowels, and all that."

"Ew!" Deborah pulled back.

"Yeah, *ew*!" parroted Blow Torch Borch. "You're the bowels, not us."

I only winced. A literate teaching professional knows that no intact *homo sapiens* can "be the bowels." I gestured to my seated colleagues and said to Deborah, "You know the gang, I think."

Deborah skimmed a negligent glance across the table. "Sure." Then she inclined her face to my ear and whispered, *"Can we step outside?"*

We entered a corridor ghostly quiet, as students were either in the cafeteria or at recess.

THE CHESTERFIELD HOURS

"So where's 'young Carrie'?" Deborah said before I could shut the door behind us.

Internally I checked up at this, like a battlefield horse scenting blood. But by will I made my feet move, and with my hand at her back I pressed her toward the front entrance.

"Where's friend Hoepplewhite?" I countered, playing it more low-down perhaps than I ought. Hoepplewhite was done for, and done with, and grotty as the whole affair had been, as a gentleman I had vowed always to ascribe the guilt to that jackal rather than to my wife.

"Don't try turning the tables," Deborah said. "Where have you stashed the little b---- ?"

"Steady on, dear." I heard the faculty door open behind us.

"Hey Chest," called Larry Berkowitz, who stood in the doorway holding a Styrofoam bowl. "Remember Carrie's soup. She's a bear when she doesn't get it."

Carrie Hahn wouldn't know how to be a bear, or a weasel, minx or muskrat. Carrie Hahn was an angel of Providence.

I bluffed a chortle even as I glared daggers at Larry. "Nice try, you rascal! You and Miss Hahn aren't fooling anyone."

It was asking too much that Larry, on blundering into the good old sex wars, should take a hint. He walked up to us and put the soup to me. "Seriously," he said. "I figured with the interruption you forgot."

"Oh, all right," I said. "I'll play up, you dog."

"Thank you so much, Larry," Deborah icily said. "To paraphrase Deep Throat, I will follow the soup."

Larry retreated in bafflement, perhaps in fear she'd vaporize him with death rays from the eyes. I'd have heartily approved it.

THE CHESTERFIELD HOURS

YOUNG VILLAIN COMES IN HANDY

Bloody rotten soup! Dicey as this was, how really like a nightmare to have Deborah stalking these halls, I held the crucial advantage of home turf. Carrie Hahn, I knew, was ensconced in her classroom in the rear wing. If I could nudge Deborah onward toward the front –

"Well, hello Chesterfields! What a wonderful sight this is!"

Fay Muck, the building principal, was a former special education teacher. Her logic betrayed a possible associative damage, as her delight now at seeing Chesterfields, plural, followed on a daily dismay at seeing Chesterfield the one.

"Why, Ms. Muck. So good of you to remember Deborah."

La Muck, with a frozen smile plastered on, looked for an anxious instant back and forth between us.

"How's your husband?" Deborah said without interest.

I cleared my throat. Le Muck, a degenerate gambler of the Dominic-customer sort, had been hoofed out by La.

"Who knows? Who cares?" Fay Muck issued an unnerving screech-owl laugh.

"Well," I said. The soup cooled in my hands.

"I hear ya," Deborah said to Muck.

Hear what? I could swear I heard my own self aspersed, with that little taunt. What if I were just to slip the soup to Muck, without a word, as if it were a Neil Diamond CD, and simply walk away? That would extricate me from both hussies at a stroke, though it might leave them assessing my sanity, and tenure loopholes…

"Ah, look at the time," I said instead. "Must retrieve my tribe from lunch."

Speaking of, here came the worst of the lot, the felonious Dylan Czarnecki, escorted by and brawling with a luckless cafeteria aide.

Deborah gave me a savage look. "Aren't you forgetting your little errand?" she said with open malice, as if Fay Muck were in Bulgaria.

This tepid soup would light the way to dusty death…

Dylan Czarnecki, bless his bestial heart, picked this moment to throw an elbow that caught the poor aide on the collarbone and gave her a good rattle. The brawlers were fifteen feet from us, and closing.

Fay Muck, back from Bulgaria, bellowed "Hey! You!"

Out, out…

I waded into the brawl and, just as Czarnecki flailed his arm round, pitched the bowl's blood-red contents onto the young villain. Judging that I'd made a good show of receiving not dealing aggression, I spun in the same motion just far enough to whip some dregs onto Deborah. A pleasing red spatter dashed her white tights.

As my wife howled oaths to blanch a wharf rat, I played it out for Fay Muck.

"Leave him to me!" I barked, clamping Dylan by the neck, at which the filthy bugger went starched and straight like Mrs. Dalloway's sheets.

"You can't touch me!" raged the hulking, reeking, girl-tormenting dunce as I bore him on toward the office, with Muck and Deborah immersed in red puddles behind me.

THE CHESTERFIELD HOURS

"You're for the jug-house now," I told Dylan Czarnecki. "A week's suspension at the least." A classroom cleansed of strife and B.O., an idyllic week of happy sixth graders all below the age of consent...

That soup was a stone that killed two birds. Carrie Angel...

STRANGE JOY

"About your soup."

Carrie Hahn turned to face me, and as she did her glossy brown hair, cut just above the shoulders, danced and swung like a silk scarf cast to the breeze.

"What soup?" she said poker-faced. Then she smiled as if complicit in its destruction. She knew what soup, and saw I hadn't it, and so it didn't exist, and so was past going into. She was like that.

I eased my way gingerly into her *kinderlair*, where everything it seemed was below the knees. On the walls were photos of Venice, of Paris, of the Great Barrier Reef; a giant calendar encircled by photos of her students; and photos of Cyrus, the yellow lab Carrie had spoken of. I warmly thought of my Daisy… but were dog introductions the done thing with a maiden colleague?

"Looks like I owe you a lunch," I said. "How's Sunday?"

She met me halfway amongst the tiny desks. I towered nearly a foot above her, but in black cord pants and pink cotton turtleneck she stood before me in a comfortable expectancy.

"Actually, I think I'll eat before then," she said. It was Tuesday.

I gave the point. "Right. Thing is, my parents make a Sunday brunch that I and my friends stop at all the time. They've been wanting you brought round… and of course Larry."

She looked shyly down and smiled. "Of course Larry. That would be lovely."

"About my dad," I intoned portentously.

"Is he British?"

"Oh no. He's a retired Marine captain. Thing is -- "

"That's so weird," she said.

"Not so weird really. What's weird is he'll want to seduce you."

"Excuse me?"

"Right. But no cost. Just tell him to stuff it and all's jolly."

"Ooh-kay. And your mom?"

"She's British."

Carrie Hahn chucked me on the breastbone. "That's not what I'm getting at!"

I absorbed this wee blow as if it were a falling rose petal. "Let us say," I said, "that my folks are tolerant of eccentricities, above all each other's."

"You and Larry better defend my honor," she said.

The sweet play of this brought me nearly to gasp with strange joy. But a Ffoulkes/Chesterfield can wear the mask...

"Do bring Cyrus," I said, "as we're all dog people. You can turn him loose on Dad if need be." I turned toward the door.

"So about my soup," she said, chaffing me, returning playfully to prologue.

"My wife's wearing it," I said, and ducked out into the hall.

I heard her say "Oh my god!" and something unintelligible, decrescendoing, as I hurried back to my happy tribe.

CONVERSATIONS

"So about my soup."

What it amounted to was that we had begun The Conversation, the one that goes on for ever and ever...

I had a steak grilling on the back porch, and Daisy back from our walk and chowing, when the phone rang. It was the evening of Bloody (Soup) Tuesday.

"Hello."

"I'll give you the dry-cleaning bill when I see you Saturday," Deborah said.

"By all means the bill, dear. But what's Saturday?"

"We're going out to dinner at La Boucherie. Then back to your place."

"Back to our house, I think you mean," I amended, out of propriety not ardor. Where had that gone?

"The day will come to sort all that out. I like the sound of 'back to your place.'" Deborah, with her speed-dating and God knew what else, liked the sounds of a lot of rummy things these days.

"Well," I said, "if you can't do better."

"I know *you* can't," Deborah said.

***

THE CHESTERFIELD HOURS

You could almost, in the pithy phrasing of Mr. T, pity the fool. The bulky, muscle-bound body had degraded to a thrashing of crutches and white plaster, the bull neck and coppery head bobbing like a turkey's...

Running with Daisy through an urban district of little shops and coffee bars, I pulled up to see this creature attempt to mount the SUV with the LOCK IN vanity plates.

Hoepplewhite, who all along had been short and stout, was quite the little tea-pot now, with left arm and right leg in casts.

I was far from gloating. Rather, I spoke because one doesn't run from this.

"Well, Hoepplewhite." As I said this, Daisy growled.

My old foe ignored me as he reached awkwardly across his body to the truck door and almost fell.

"F---! Piece of s---!" Finally he looked at me, and his face contorted. "What do you want?"

Daisy and I stood easy. Pity in fact did not come, but neither did spite or gladness. "Not a thing," I said. "It's a shame, really it is. How you coming?"

Hoepplewhite leaned back against the truck, as if to rest before the final assault on the stupidly high driver's seat.

"Not as bad as you think, pal. I got Jeanine coming over to cook and clean and throw me a bang every few days."

"Ah," was all I said.

"Hey, your slut of a wife says she's gone back to you."

"Has she?" Perhaps Deborah found this useful. Perhaps she believed it true...

I jingled Daisy's leash and walked away. Wait a minute, I thought. The villain wants thrashing, for what he said just now about Deborah. Oh never mind…

"I'll be back," Hoepplewhite called after me. "Count on it."

"Come the fine day you're top 'o the world," I tossed back, "tell it to your old ma. Don't bother me."

THE CHESTERFIELD HOURS

FORTUNE AND INTIMACY

Deborah was a very desirable woman. Our intimacy, which against the tenor of the times I discussed with no one, had been intense. Certainly it had gnawed within me through all the unquiet nights since our parting. But she had waited a fatal tad long to insinuate her lovely self back into my nights – and a single measly Saturday night at that. I wanted none of it. I wanted…

But no gentleman, only a swine, subjects a woman to the indignity of divorce. He is at her disposal, and must lump the consequences. So what was to be done about this ghastly dinner date, which cast such a pall upon the fresh-dawn Sunday brunch to follow?

"About my soup."

When I replied *"My wife's wearing it,"* I was fleeing the room but hardly The Conversation. It is a biggish disclosure for a gentleman to tell a maiden she is linked by physical substance to the gentleman's wife. Even in such fallen times as these, the better sort of maiden, like Carrie Hahn, will react. And so – *"Oh my god!"* – The Conversation lived.

***

If I could survive to Sunday.

Bryng!

"Hello."

"My dear," my mother Daphne said, "your father's just beside himself with anticipation."

"Well, if the self he's beside wears a skirt, it's in trouble."

"Is your new friend really ready for this?"

"She's bringing her dog, Mother. A big one."

"Oh goody."

"It is goody, as we know that even at sixty-six Dad reckons he's got five appendages still too dear to lose."

"Right," Daphne said. "I don't suppose he'll be pushing on through the dog."

In the event she was still dubious, I said, "Well, for all his talk he never veered hard toward Deborah, and I'm no attack dog."

"Now, darling, you are positively a killer and no mistake. It's why Deborah will never let you go."

Saturday night's prospective "hook-up" came back to me with a revolting and forcible clap.

"Speaking of Deborah, and mistakes – I trust, Mother, that there'll be no Fortune talk on Sunday."

"Pish posh," she said. "I haven't had three Manhattans since your rehearsal dinner."

"Can you assure me, then," I said, "that mimosas on Sunday won't produce another infamous result?"

Only listen to yourself, I suddenly thought. You are presuming of Carrie Hahn either something monstrous or unconscionably premature. It was panic rising… it was the dinner date!

"Have you considered, dear," Daphne said, "that Deborah might actually desire your person more than she does my mother's alleged money?"

"Then back to your place." It was just thinkable…

***

Then again, Deborah might not want or require full possession of my person -- merely its one-night's rental.

Bryng!

"Hello."

Deborah directly said, "I wasn't as gracious as I might have been the other night."

I had been reading, Daisy on the couch with me, her head in my lap.

"Don't give it a thought, dear," I said.

"No, honestly. And my saying you can't do better – that was uncalled for."

"Not called for by me, certainly."

"My belief is you'd do damn well, and so will I."

I took note of her choice of tense. "Ah," was all I said.

She let a moment pass. Then she said, "Have you never felt any paternal stirrings since we first got together?"

"You know I did have," I said, fixing my own verb tense with care. The immemorial way of the Ffoulkes was to bear one child to a generation: Victoria, Daphne, next myself, who had been only too ready to do my happy duty from the day I married Deborah. But she had put it off…

"If you say so," she said. "Maybe you should have pressed the issue."

This casual revisionism bore with it a whiff of evil. "I'm sure it's for the best," I said.

I heard only the faint intake of her breath. Then: "How dare you."

"You propose to be the speed dating mother of my children? Thank you, no."

"Who are you, Prufrock?" she said. "Let's just take it as it comes for a while. Saturday night is going to be hot. Promise."

"I shall wear my trousers rolled," I said, and rang off. The woman who next unrolls 'em, I thought, will be the woman who's in for keeps. As I was, and will be.

***

Presumably Deborah wanted to roll, and unroll, once a fortnight or so, then leave like a thief. And get a baby in the bargain. And a chunk of The Fortune down the line.

Thank you, no.

I woke up shaking in the night. I hung fire, with eyes burning, till five a.m., when my guv'nor habitually rose. My call was picked up after two rings.

"Semper Fidelis."

"When was the last time you played hero?" I said.

"Never."

"Not during Tet? Not in the Delta?"

"All the heroes are dead."

I shifted tacks. "How'd you like to be Deborah's hero?"

This produced a pause. "I think she's immune to my charms. Though I'd get a small piece of her on Christmas Eve."

"The mistletoe being your pretext, streets from where she stood."

"Like with hand grenades, close enough."

"Dad," I said, "this Saturday night I may be called to battle."

"Yes?"

"Right. Now, a French restaurant is not the Mekong. But villains may appear."

"Hoepplewhite? He ran from you once."

"Evil could wear any face this night."

"Where's Deborah in this?" Captain Jack said.

"It's her you'll be there for. If I go down, you look to her, not me."

"Time and place?"

"La Boucherie, eight o'clock. Lie low till the fur flies."

"Check."

GETTING BIFFED TO MAKE A BUCK

I had won four hundred dollars from the mob bookie Dominic, in the same Super Bowl intrigue that finally broke Hoepplewhite. The typical thirty-two year-old American male would have long since spent the winnings on a Callaway driver or satellite radio. But a Ffoulkes/Chesterfield is provident.

"You'll have earned it," I told Larry Berkowitz, as I handed him four crisp C-notes in the faculty room. "Remember you'll likely get biffed, but we men were meant to bleed. We never win or keep our women else, and that's what we're putting next in your future, once this campaign is won."

"I won't let you down," Larry said.

"I know you won't," I said. "Carrie of course must be spared the baser details."

"But she wants them."

"Stellar girl."

"She's curious about your wife."

I felt a tingle of panic at this, a sense of dipping the old toe into the Rubicon. I looked to the end of the table, where Grime Bat and Blow Torch, having noticed the cash exchange, goggled at us.

"Tell Carrie I need her," I said to Larry. "That is, I really need her to play it out."

"You tell her."

I stood. This was getting nearish.

"I can't," was all I said, and I left the room.

THE CHESTERFIELD HOURS

SHOWDOWN AT LA BOUCHERIE

La Boucherie was one of those sort of compromised French places with a menu mostly in English. That is as it should be. It will not do for those fellows to come seeking one's custom in one's own land, and pretend they're running the Tour D'Argent.

Deborah and I stepped out of a gusty March night, exchanged *bon soirs* with the maitre d', and advanced to the young gentleman checking coats.

Deborah let the boy tug her coat off from behind.

Well, I never, Trevor...

Her dress was a glossy and luxuriant kelly green, cut lower than underthings could be devised to, well, underlie. The cleavage, real and spectacular, was simply the Western Front, Flanders to Switzerland. A sensationally lurid ruby pendant menaced from above, seeking specific gravity.

"Lovely, dear."

One might assume an acculturated, if not born, gentleman to be little moved by sheer female splendor. If the gentleman is *moi*, one would be wrong.

"Thanks." Deborah knew well enough that understatement in me was no sign of indifference.

We were seated. With every gesture, with every breath, every glance and physical inclination, Deborah rippled, crested, flowed like seductive tropical waves. She washed over me, and my pulse hammered in my veins. Ten weeks now…

We settled into a bottle of cabernet. Deborah reached across the table, dipping provocatively, and clinked my glass.

"To life," she said.

"Flashing before me," I replied, wrenching my gaze, with effort, upwards into her eyes.

The restaurant had one largeish dining room and a smaller, darker room for the bar. Facing that small room, I could see the customers' side of the bar, dark wood and richly varnished. Occasionally the bartender's sleeve, white and cufflinked, would snake out from behind the entrance wall. Standing at the bar was a large man, about my height of six-foot one, but bulkier. He wore a handsome loden jacket, white shirt and tie, and an enormous Borsalino hat that obscured much of his face. Standing with a bottle and aperitif glass, he suggested an amalgam of Luca Brasi, and a gunslinger with his red-eye.

Deborah had one elbow on the table, and held her wine glass so its base nearly touched one breast. "Our life together," she said, "was lovely in so many ways."

"Was it?" I saw the big man at the bar put an index finger to the side of his nose, a pointless sign of acknowledgment.

"Absolutely," Deborah said. "Wouldn't it be liberating – in the truest sense – to take from life its most instinctual joys, and reject its institutional rot and moralistic preachings?"

"Ah," I said. "The mind-forged manacles. Dicky old stuff like marriage, duty, the rule of law." I gulped at my wine.

She tipped forward again and touched my hand with her free one. "You are an instinctual man. I know that."

In thrall to her murmurous voice, her too-perfect flesh and flowery scent, I was beginning to have "ideas." I drained my glass.

Deborah was saying that "non-conformists" were generally grey and grotty little cranks whom one can only pity and avoid. But if one has worldly station, and means, and looks and taste, one should be able to take of the world's pleasures, and keep only those traditions that make sense and augment pleasure, without guilt or fear of stigma.

"I am your lover," she concluded, "and your pleasure. We don't belong sharing a bathroom and knocking into each other around the kitchen."

Isn't it Milton's Satan, I wondered, who becomes the mist, the foe who enters where he will and can't be fenced out? Or is cabernet the mist, into which all my principles as a gentleman will dissolve? My head reeled. Bosoms the mist...

"Geez Louise," Deborah said. "Enjoy the wine, but pace yourself."

"Right," I said, and put the bottle back down. "The night is young, and all that." *Back to your place.* If I surrender to this mist, be it liquid or flesh, I will, in Churchill's words, go to hell as soon as there is vacant passage.

At that moment, Larry Berkowitz and Carrie Hahn walked in. Both carried coats to their table thirty feet from ours, nearer to the small room and bar. So Larry, with four hundred iron men from me in his pocket, had cheaped out and stiffed the coat-check lad.

Jack Chesterfield wouldn't know Carrie and Larry from Adam and Eve, while Deborah of course knew only Larry. I had to finesse this...

"Why, the confounded ass," I said to Deborah. "Berkowitz has brought his date here."

"What?"

"Hasn't had a date since his junior prom. Said he'd got one for this weekend. I mentioned we were coming here. I mean, can you believe it?"

"Surely you didn't invite him," Deborah said, as she studied the couple, coats draped over their chairs, who looked more sibling than romantic in attitude.

"Good God, no," I said. "I never dreamed. He's pretty assy in the social graces, but I never conceived he'd blunder in here."

"He's looking around," Deborah said. "There he sees us!"

"Courage, dear." Suavely I raised my empty wine glass and saluted Berkowitz who squinted dumbly at us. I mouthed "Cheers," and immediately turned back to Deborah.

"That'll freeze 'em for now," I said. "They've been acknowledged, and politely cut. We'll stop at their table just briefly between dinner and coffee."

"Well handled," Deborah said. "What would possess that idiot to come here?"

"He's a great soul but not confident. My guess is that our coming here is to him both a seal of approval and a security blanket if things start downhill with the girl."

"She's cute enough," Deborah said. "Dressed like that she's not his hired tart."

Carrie Hahn sat with her hands in her lap and never looked at us. She wore a calf-length black wool skirt, a long-sleeved white blouse, stockings and two-inch heels. With a tasteful gold necklace she resembled a slightly racy nun.

"She's fine," I said (I hoped neutrally). Larry on the other hand could not have been less fine for La Boucherie, looking like a dentist on poker night in cardigan sweater and Dockers.

The Borsalino man had noticed my toast to Larry, and from under his black brim stared at the new couple. Perhaps he was wondering: *What villains?*

For my part I wondered, in the words of that Pink vixen so beloved of my lesser-achieving female sixth-graders: *What is going to get this party started?*

Larry, so the aggressor in his fantasies and at his keyboard, was his usual passive public self now, sipping at his water while Carrie Hahn stole a bestranded look at Deborah and me.

"I say, Robert," I called, catching the waiter who had so operatically sung out his name to us. "Send by me a drink to our friends over there. A half-bottle of this excellent cabernet for the lady, and a double Seven and Seven for the gentleman."

Larry, I knew, had very poor and unhappy brains for drinking. If I could fasten but one cup upon him...

"Can we forget them?" Deborah said. "At least till after dinner?"

"Forget whom?" I said, and forced a smile. At the memory of Carrie Hahn's winsome and forgiving *"What soup?"* my smile became less faked and genuinely fond. Then I caught myself. Deborah, of course, would wish such fondness to derive from her own charms.

And it is to be remembered that those charms were acting very powerfully on Chesterfield the organism. *Back to your place.* The resort to excitable syrups, the sending of whisky drowned in soda pop to catalyze the slug Berkowitz, was all to prevent my winging to perdition in the arms of this seductive stranger my wife…

While Larry's potion took effect there was nothing for it but to concentrate on Deborah.

"Do you have any idea," she said, slightly panting, "what I'm going to do with you back at your place?"

Conceive triplets, I feared, considering the mist of fertility wafting off her, which roused me in like kind.

In the next room, the Borsalino man looked slightly dejected as time stuck and no hostilities threatened.

What *was* Berkowitz thinking? But, I thought gloomily, it's all my own muck-up. One can't ask an inward-type, wallflower lad to pull off a mock date *and* a mock fight in one evening when he hasn't done either in his lifetime for real…

Deborah was saying, "I'd love to play with Daisy, but please don't let's touch her when we get back to your place. Do put her out."

My desire to check the other table, and young Carrie, was like a furious itch, yet I allowed Deborah's brown eyes to continue devouring mine. As soon as she looked to her wine glass, I shot a fast glance over. As I returned my gaze to Deborah, the surreal image I retained, which must have been a trick of the mind's eye, was of Carrie Hahn taking a stevedore's slug from Larry's Seven and Seven…

"What're *you* lookin' at?"

If this at last was Berkowitz' challenge, he was by way of throwing his voice through a gutter strumpet. But when I looked back over I saw the same back of Larry's head I'd seen before. Carrie Hahn meanwhile was drilling me with her own eyes.

"Yeah, you!" she said. "You think buyin' me a drink gives you the right to look me over like a piece of meat?"

"Excuse me?" Deborah said.

"I… I assure you, miss," I said, "I meant no such thing."

Carrie looked to Larry and said, "Go take care of it."

Snapping to the new paradigm, I rose in my chair. I must needs be no wildman, simply put myself in range.

Larry, never a quick snapper, sat befuddled, looking back and forth between Carrie and me.

"I said, take care of the guy," Carrie told him, even more sinisterly.

I had already rejected cartoon aggression in my own performance. Something else must bring Larry out of his chair. I advanced on him and kept my eyes off Carrie.

"It's all a nothing, old man," I said. "Let's shake on it."

"Get back here!" Deborah called, but I pressed ahead.

Larry stood. We clasped hands. I put an arm round Larry's shoulders and whispered, *"If you've got one punch in you for a lifetime, by the living God throw it now!"*

Larry, four inches shorter, with the build of an uncoordinated spider, waved a paw that nestled against my jaw, and I straightaway crashed to the floor.

"Oh my God!" Deborah shrieked.

"Sacred Blue!" Robert the waiter wailed.

"That'll show him!" Carrie Hahn said.

THE CHESTERFIELD HOURS

I decided that Larry's *papier-mache* punch should have done me inner-ear damage, so that I could raise up, survey the field, whisper commands if need be, then flop again. My model was Trevor Berbick, who in effect had been knocked out three times by one Mike Tyson punch.

I pushed myself up with one arm and hissed to Larry, *"Put a hundred on the table to pay for yourself."* The remaining three hundred, I thought as I swooned back to the floor, you'll be earning directly. You poor sod...

Payday, apocalyptic as all our yesterdays, arrived with Jack Chesterfield. Larry simply disappeared behind great loden shoulders and the black Borsalino. Next I saw him flying through the air before a wall intervened.

"Son," Jack said. "Can you hear me?"

"Leave me, damn you!" I said, splaying myself like a man fallen from a ladder. "Get Deborah out of here!"

My guv'nor had had a solid half hour to get a load of Deborah and didn't need telling twice. But a good soldier before scooping up the Sabines will first ensure the enemy is out of commission. Captain Jack seized a limpish Larry...

"Unhand him!" I whispered. *"He's a pal. Shove off!"*

Next day at brunch, Larry, fingering his lumps, would say that it was no worse than I'd promised, and a sight more pleasant and profitable than professional review by Fay Muck...

Perhaps fifteen seconds had elapsed. Jack was steering Deborah to the door. Larry was the pulverised heap that I only affected to model. Carrie Hahn was standing over me, a goddess looking down on the fools that mortals be.

She said, "I'm so sor -- "

"Stash that bloody wine bottle in your coat," I said. "It's paid for and wasting." I'd retrieve my own coat next day, in the event Deborah hadn't it up already by then on eBay.

I leaped to my feet and took Carrie's hand. "Let's go," I said.

"But Larry -- "

" ...will be right on time for brunch."

We took the Goodfellas tour through the bowels of the brasserie. Wait staff, and *sous chefs* in filthy white, scattered clucking like barnyard chickens as Carrie and I dashed through and out the back.

We emerged into an alley that felt greasy beneath the shoes. I peeked round a corner out to the street. Captain Jack had one arm over Deborah's luminous bare shoulders, his opposite hand on her hip, bearing her toward his car. When I heard them roar off, I gently tugged at Carrie's hand, and we stepped out into the street.

We stood under a street light and studied one another. Her eyes were bright but I saw a question forming.

Thinking fast I said, "You've saved my bacon," and chuckled. "Larry froze, eh?"

She wasn't having it. "It was... fun. But you were at dinner with your wife."

No running from this. "A terrible summons which I answered out of duty alone. Do you accept my word as a gentleman on that?"

She stepped close to me. The bottle in her coat lodged between us.

"I do," she said.

A breeze swept down the street, the first in five months that seemed to come from someplace warm and habitable.

"I say, does your Cyrus take it hard when you leave him home alone?"

"Oh my God. He's an absolute bear." She circled an arm round mine, and we began to walk.

"Daisy too, doubtless ripping my stuffings out as we speak." I enmeshed Carrie's fingers in my own. "Let's go collect both hellhounds and walk 'em together. Boy, girl, boy, girl, what?"

And so breaks the long unquiet winter...

"Date," Carrie Hahn said. "I'll show you the way back to my place."

The breeze, the girl... no talk of a fortune that might or might not be. She's looking at *you*, mate, not at *it*.

Which makes her, for good and for keeping, your fortune that is.

END BOOK ONE

Book Two

FAREWELL THE BIG WARS

THE CHESTERFIELD HOURS

Part One

THE SIN OF CHASTITY

What next, then? I had already faced out the blackest infamy a gentleman can endure. My nemesis Benedict Hoepplewhite was sunk by his own goatish attempts to out-paramour the Turk. Deborah, though still alluring, had lost her most dangerous power, possession of my heart. Carrie Hahn was the best that ever they come, and she loved me as I loved her. With that, you have won out, wealth and fame be damned.

Now, I've said there would be skirmishes, even in peacetime. But what if peace itself should prove an illusion?

Well, I was still then a naïve lad. Relaxed now, I decided it was a time for pals, for the shoring up of their ruins...

"You say we men are meant to bleed," said Larry Berkowitz the following week in the faculty room. "So I've bled already all over my best sweater. Now how about getting me laid?"

"Damn your eyes," I said. "D'you take me for a bloody pimp? If I could I wouldn't put you with a decent maiden, until you talk and act like a gentleman."

Larry slumped. "You're right. I'm an a--hole."

Directly I felt remorse. I'd never have got past the treachery of Hoepplewhite and Deborah without Carrie and Larry. I put a hand on Larry's shoulder.

"No, you're only a clot-poll, and that's curable since it doesn't go as deep as the heart."

"Thanks. So cure me."

Given my chaste relation to Carrie Hahn, I was presently, in carnal matters, physician without practice. But I have won, I reminded myself. I have won the big war.

"Listen," I said, "you don't go a-trolling for rosebuds, you go a-maying. Let Carrie and me help you, and be patient."

Larry lowered his voice, but with the clot-poll's spasmic modulation. "I'd still kinda like to get laid." The next "lowering" was into a crashing stage whisper: *"I never have been, you know."*

The door behind us gently swung open, but no one turned to it due to a great vulgar eruption of laughter down the end of the table. *"Mwah-haha-enh-enh-enh-enh-enh! Nyah-ha-ha-ha-haaahh!"*

Blow Torch Borch and Grime Bat Grimmboat cast looks of malicious glee toward Larry and myself.

"What a coupla losers," Blow Torch said. "The blind leading the blind."

Grime Bat addressed me now. "Yeah, check back with us when you actually get some yourself, okay, pal?"

This frightful allusion could not have been more cruelly timed. In the doorway stood a stricken Carrie Hahn, reddening from the cheeks to the ears.

"Come in, dolling," Blow Torch rasped. "We were just tawking about you."

But Carrie had bolted the room.

I was on my feet. "Unnatural hags!" I said. "In a better day for your race and our nation, you'd have done the Dolly for this lad, and made for him an 'ebrew match that's fruitful and enduring."

"Be careful what you wish for," Grime Bat said. "If you get on our bad side we'll tell Carrie to dump you and take geek-o here. Isn't her father a Jew?"

I sighed. "I don't know. I wouldn't think of asking." I went out the door and down the hall after Carrie.

***

She had a smile as well as tears on her lovely oval face as she turned to my entrance. The tears were well underway, the smile belated; it came in fact from my tripping, as usual, on the low-lying debris left by her kindergarteners.

"Blast!" I said, regaining my balance. "My father had less danger of Bouncing Betties in Nam than I from what your little blighters lay for me."

"A slight exaggeration," she said, "as your father would be quick to point out. And you know you love my kids."

My near-pratfall had somewhat broken her mortification. Mindful of graphic PDAs during school hours, I took both her hands.

"Are the little people actually here with us, and I not knowing it? Everything's below the waist here."

"Except me," she said, and kissed both my hands.

I was yet a married gentleman, and she a gentle maiden, and so there was no talk of…

THE CHESTERFIELD HOURS

Well, in fact there is no talk. It is a fantastic misconception of contemporary Americans, who talk and talk, that gentlefolk are ones more for talk than for action. As shown with my hooligan in the park, in dust-ups at Ripped & Shredded and at La Boucherie (at which young Carrie singularly distinguished herself), the gentled are first for action... and for no talking about it. What's talked is mere social lubrication...

"Come, wipe thine eyes and forget those biddies," I said. "The good years shall devour them ere they make us weep."

With our hands enmeshed she pulled us tight together.

"Oh!"

"Sorry, love. That's a pencil point you feel."

The coast was clear, and we kissed. "That's 64 Crayolas I feel," she said, "to put a blunter point on it."

"Awfully glad to see you, the whole lot of them."

"Just awfully," she said. "Magenta, Flesh, and all those rascals." She sweetly pulled back from me by inches. Her tears were drying and she wore too little make-up to smear.

I needed to get my class back from lunch. I captured Carrie to me once more.

"Give me my sin again," I said, and kissed her good-bye.

BUBBLES LA MUCK

Granny Victoria was dead. How could a dog, a horse, a rat have life, and she no breath at all?

Well, Granny had after all been ninety-one. But my mum Daphne's mother, matriarch of the Ffoulkes, had seemed immortal, so for Ffoulkes and Chesterfields alike the world had changed. And to certain interested parties not of the blood, it meant the Fortune game again was afoot.

"Look, you men, she simply doesn't belong now," Daphne said after the service. "I mean to say, I adored Deborah as my own daughter until she did the dirty on our boy here."

Her boy, I Chesterfield, was fixing himself a whisky and soda three feet away. We were at my parents' modest bungalow, greeting friends and relatives at the post-funeral get-together.

"Let her come with bells on," my father Jack said, looking out with Daphne at the brazen latest arrival. "She's never looked better, and I've got to have something to get me through this parade of fools and fossils."

"Oh, take a day off, you beastly old lech."

Carrie Hahn had attended the service and properly gone on home. Deborah, though still my legal wife, was a bit pushing it by showing up here. But there was her new red sports car pulling onto the actual lawn.

"Well, Dad," I said, turning to the guv'nor, whisky in hand. "I'd say to get through it with a couple stiff belts, whilst giving Deborah the ozone."

"He's cut off, my dear," Daphne said. "As of this minute."

Captain Jack only grunted.

Larry Berkowitz, adrift amongst strangers, floated up.

"Jesus, here comes your wife. Since La Boucherie she must hate my guts."

With a studied negligence I took a pull on my whisky. "If you existed for her she might. Courage, old man. She's not one of your video vampiresses."

In the time it took to have this exchange and pour Larry a ginger ale, Deborah made her entrance, and a queen's beeline to my parents. Daphne waited for Deborah to extend a hand before she took it, and suffered Deborah's kiss on the cheek without reciprocation.

Daphne, of course, was the new possessor of The Fortune – if it existed. Next in line, myself – again if there was more than a rumour to inherit. Deborah's awareness of The Fortune was acute, her belief in it absolute. And Jack's place in all this?

"My hero!" Deborah cooed, embracing the brawny sixty-six year old Captain the second Daphne turned a back to her.

The hero of La Boucherie she meant, though Carrie Hahn in fact had saved that situation. Jack in lugging Deborah and her cleavage out onto the street had merely served his own lascivious pleasure, as in days of yore he'd served the nation.

Deborah knew not to show all that top-flesh today, but in this her coarser phase she simply pushed up from the bottom, matching tasteful blouse and blazer with a skimpy black mini-skirt.

"Come to Papa." Jack enveloped his daughter-in-law in great arms, one hand, for poise weight no doubt, on the upper rise of her buttocks.

"Oh, really now," Daphne said. "I think I may vom."

She took my hand and led me aside. Larry trailed puppishly after, until Daphne buzzed him off with a laser glance.

We relocated against a wall, from which point we could survey the full field. My building principal, Fay Muck, arrived looking appropriately if uncharacteristically muted. Larry, cast adrift again by Daphne's glare, was pounced on by La Muck as a lifebuoy in an ocean of strangers. That's a reprieve, I thought.

"I say, Mother, that was a bit truculent by your standard. Surely we can all get along today at least."

Daphne had her rocks Usual going, and took a gulp. "You naive fool! And I took you for a clear-eyed Ffoulkes." She stared at her husband pouring out a glass of wine for Deborah.

"Steady on," I said. "Which number Manhattan is that you're working on there?" Three, for Daphne, would mean that chaos was come again...

"Don't you just worry about it, sonny," she shot back.

"I know she's not the girl I married, Mother, but it's behind me. And you've always been pretty indulgent of Dad's peccadilloes."

Daphne's aspect brightened, exaggeratedly. "Fancy a drink yourself, dear?"

"Got one, Mother. As you see."

She snatched the whisky from my hand and slammed it down on an end table.

"Oh, but that's not your fare. Methinks you have a great desire to a bottle of hay, for you are an ass-headed idiot!" She huffed out of the room.

THE CHESTERFIELD HOURS

Fay Muck was well-tuned already. Larry stood next her with a champagne bottle, pouring liberally, as one does with the good old gas can into the lawnmower. So formidable was she, sober, that a sozzled Muck could only be easier soil.

"Oh, Mr. Chesterfield!" La Muck sang out. "My heart goes out to you! She must have been a great lady!"

"Quite." I had my whisky back, for a sort of armor.

"I could swear your wife snubbed me a minute ago," Fay Muck said, a bit of the old edge returning.

"Let me top that off for you," Larry said, quick-drawing the champagne.

"I'm sure you're mistaken, Ms. Muck," I said. "She's just quite shattered, you know."

Across the room Deborah played with my guv'nor's shirt buttons whilst he whispered in her ear, his nose in her auburn hair.

"Pretty bubbles!" La Muck said, holding the freshened glass beneath her own nose. Presumably she had not come to dance on Granny's grave, but when in Rome…

"Well," I said, "as Mother's gone out, I'll see to the kitchen."

"I'll help!" Larry said, but Fay Muck caught him by the collar as she would a delinquent sixth-grader.

"Not so fast, you little devil," she said, yanking Larry back.

"You know," she said to me, "if my lousy husband had drunk half as much, and I twice as much, we might have had a f---ing marriage after all."

At this I took my leave. I'd rather not be where Deborah and Muck rampaged like Godzilla and Mothra, laying waste not the world's great cities but rather its male fools and fossils.

NATHANIEL

Thus I saw to the kitchen by way of walking straight through it and out the back door. There was no sign anywhere of Daphne, but surely she must remember her duty at some point and return to it.

Well, it wasn't a patch on me, as I judged I'd done my own true duty at church and graveside. Funeral orgies, as Mark Twain called 'em, are either empty bollocks or the seventh rung of Hades. A gentleman doesn't truck with either. I got in my car and drove home.

I changed to polo shirt and khakis, and as Daisy capered round me, picked up the phone.

"Hello," Carrie Hahn said.

"I'm AWOL from the most godawful drunken scrum. Daisy wants walking, and I wonder if you and your Cyrus would like to catch us on the hop."

"I'm kind of in the middle of something here."

This was so unexpected as to bear a whiff of menace.

"Everything quite all right?"

"Yes, really," she said, uncomfortably. "Can I call you later?"

I weighed tact versus surety. A gentleman does not exist in the world without the former. The latter must exist at all times for those he loves.

"Tell you what," I said. "I'll just give Daisy a sniff of it now, and we'll come by at six for a real perambulation."

"Oh... all right," Carrie said. "Six, then."

"Right," I said, ringing off, but it didn't feel right, quite.

***

There is that Edward Hopper painting, typical and atypical at once, depicting a young couple on a porch at night. Typically for Hopper, the couple's eyes do not meet, nor presumably do their present thoughts or motives. Atypically, the couple is teen-aged, not in any apparent way wounded by the world. The boy looks to her, importunate, just possibly aggressively so. The girl, nearer the door, looks ambivalent, hunted even...

I deliberately parked a block away, so that I could approach discreetly. Daisy trotted on short corgi's legs beside me as we approached the frame house where Carrie Hahn took a first-floor flat.

Accordingly, Carrie's place opened onto the front porch, and we used it for cocktails, for reading and hand-holding on the bench, for attending upon our dogs. A proper porch is a good old thing.

Today was looking a little Hopperish. As I walked up with Daisy, I first saw a shaggy brown-haired head that once was common but which has lost fashion... oh, call it Kennedyish. Boys do not look like Kennedys today.

And my first reaction was to judge him a boy. But I was by then over thirty, and Carrie Hahn, whom everyone thought looked a girl, in her twenties. One loses the years...

Carrie was seated on the bench with her yellow lab Cyrus dozing at her feet. The boy, er, young gentleman leaned against a pillar. In some impalpable sense, though, the young man hovered – importunately.

"Evening," I called when Daisy and I reached the front walk. There is discretion for one's approach, but upon joining with actual people there

105

is nothing for it but civilised greeting. Naturally one keeps one's guard up -- discreetly.

The young man turned and straightened to attention. That is no longer "a given," as they say. Young men today do not necessarily straighten, or for that matter budge, to greet one.

"How are you, sir?" the young man said, extending a hand.

I shook it.

"Hey, girl," the young man said to Daisy, squatting to her and extending the same hand for her to sniff, lick, for that matter to shred if she took mind. But Daisy took what was offered her, and after a sniff allowed her chin stroked. At that point, she licked.

This brief sequence caused me inwardly to relax. A good nose for villains, has Daisy.

But a gentleman does not size up crucial human situations entirely upon a dog's say-so. A country gentleman might. Then again a country gentleman might give his animals no say-so whatever...

"Mr. Chesterfield," Carrie said, "this is Nathaniel. Nathaniel, meet Mr. Chesterfield."

I studied Carrie's eyes. She was not fearful, just uneasy. That was all right. Just as it would not be proper for Nathaniel to be strangling her upon the bench, it was entirely proper that we all three should feel some unease at this moment

"Very glad to meet you too, sir. Welcome to our city."

Nathaniel was shortish to me, perhaps five foot seven, but not for Carrie, who's barely over five feet. A likely enough lad, decently dressed.

"Is it so obvious," he said, "that I'm not from around here?"

I let Daisy go to her pal Cyrus, and they wagged and bumped noses. Being relieved of biological importunacy, they knew no unease in their relations.

"I assure you," I told Nathaniel, "the signifiers are all admirable."

Nathaniel had made me speak to this, thus he might now demand elaboration on the order of "Like what?" But he did not. So he was rather a blend of rudeness and breeding.

"Shall we walk these brutes of ours?" I said to Carrie.

"Of course," she said.

"I'll take Cyrus!" said Nathaniel, lurching to grab the leash that lay coiled in a porch chair.

And so we walked, the five of us. As we did so, I recalled the park in January, and hoodie-hooligan's demand: *"Who the f--- are you?"* Nathaniel was not that young man, and neither of course was I. There will be time, there will be time…

We walked. Little sound, no fury, no signifiers, nothing.

ETERNAL MANHATTAN

The night came down hard and early. One gets through an enervating episode, like a funeral, with a little foresight and the company of loved ones. But when new enervations erupt and pile upon others, one is dazed and a little battered. Add to them whisky early in the day...

Bryng! went the phone at ten that evening. I was asleep on the couch, my limp hand just ticking Daisy on the floor beneath me. Carrie must be calling, with particulars...

"Hello."

"Son," my father Jack said, "is your mother with you?"

"God no. She had a deal of cleaning up to do. Hasn't she been at it?"

"She hasn't even been here since Deb... since about two o'clock."

I heard a clinking of china. "Well, someone's back there cleaning up."

"Oh, um," he muttered. "I've got a girl helping."

"I see. Girl name of Deborah."

I was still woozy. My father hemmed and hawed something, whilst I doodled a couplet on the phone-side scratch pad:

I'm the 'usband, 'e's me pater

I steps off so's 'e can date 'er

"Damn it, boy, how are we going to get your mother back?"

"Start by not tupping her daughter-in-law. Goodnight, Dad." I blamed him for calling and not being Carrie Hahn.

When I stood, my head throbbed and I nearly lost my balance and fell over Daisy. I felt peeved with everyone, myself included, but above all I wanted to hear from Carrie Hahn.

Was this over-selfish, with a vanishing parent on my hands? Was Daphne so distraught at old Granny V ringing out? No, clearly my mother just had a mad on. It had been a bit thick, Jack's paw on Deborah's bum...

Carrie did not call. I had had a baddish sleep, and even that was now wrecked. I locked up and put out the lights. Daisy followed me upstairs. Couch to bed, bad to worse. Perchance to dream? Of bloody *what*?

***

Just a wee tinkle. No, not that. A Ffoulkes/Chesterfield prostate comes with an iron-clad nine-decade warrantee. It only goes, finally, with everything else at once.

It was a sound in the night, in the room.

Tink! Clink!

I sat up in bed. Then I reached down and felt Daisy beneath me. Her head was up, and I saw the reflection of her open eyes. She was at rest, but alert.

"Darling boy," came a voice from the door that opened to the hallway. There was a distinct form in that door, leaning against the jamb.

"Mother. Are ye fantastical, or that indeed which outwardly ye show?"

She took definition in the moonlight through the window. I saw now she held a whisky glass, which *tinkle-inkled* with ice. Her ancient family ring glinted.

"A quite familiar old lady with a fresh Manhattan. Pretty much what you've always been outwardly shown, dear."

109

"Yet fantastical somehow in one's bedroom in the dead of night," I said. "You were quite snappish all day. Now this. What's it all about, Mother?"

She glided further into the room and stood by the window. Daisy sat composed at my feet, staring at my eerie mother, who appeared bluish-white with the moonlight streaming over her. Never had she so matched her own diamond and sapphire ring.

"I 'gin to be a-weary 'o the son," she said, "more so the daughter-in-law, most of all that pestiferous husband of mine. The assy-ness of you lot!"

"But Mother, no gentleman subjects a woman to the indignity -- "

"Oh, tell that one to the Marines!"

Daphne was gliding toward the door. I fell back upon my pillow, feeling woozy, woozy...

"But," I said, exhaustion overtaking me, "but... it's you that taught me... no gentleman... "

"I," she seemed to say, "want a holiday. I am going to Europe to die. I'll post you the notice so you can carry on. Ta ta."

"But... Mother... what about The Ffff... The For... "

I fell into a deep slumber.

***

The phone rang at 6:30. I fumbled for it, feeling bleary and all-overish.

"I know you're an early riser, thank God," Carrie Hahn said.

"I am not risen," I said. "I may in fact be dead."

"Not you for self-complaint! Who *is* this?"

I sat up. "Sorry, love. It's been the strangest night."

"Most strange, indeed," she said.

"How came it so for you?" I said. "Where's Nathaniel?"

"Walking Cyrus."

"Oh monstrous."

"He spent the night on the porch, vigilling and serenading. He wanted to elope, actually."

Monstrous! "I see."

"He never crossed my threshold," she said.

"Stellar girl."

"Your mother, however, did."

"I'll be right over," I said.

HOPPER PLUS ONE

"Don't mind Nathaniel," Carrie said as I sat with her on the porch bench. "We can still talk."

"Right."

I looked at the young man who sat across from us on the porch ledge. Cyrus and Daisy, both well-walked now, sprawled in the space between us.

"My focus is on my vigil," Nathaniel said. "I have nothing against you or your mother."

"Awfully big of you," I said. I turned back to Carrie. "Mother had a drink going, did she?"

"Or against your wife," Nathaniel added.

"Yes," Carrie said to me. "Her third Manhattan. For frank speaking, she said."

"That you'll never get divorced from," Nathaniel p.p.s.-ed.

"Yet no bottle or ice supply?"

"Not that I could see," Carrie said.

"They say your wife is way smoking hot," Nathaniel said.

"Did Mother seem... alive?" I said.

"And all I ask for is Carrie," Nathaniel said.

"Well," Carrie said, "of course alive."

"Who nobody even wanted in high school," Nathaniel said.

"Nathaniel," Carrie said in a passion of fury, "go away! Leave us this minute or I'll set Cyrus on you!"

Nathaniel instead clipped the leash on Cyrus. "Cyrus loves me," he said. "Unlike some people I could name."

He turned to me. "Want me to take Daisy too?"

"Decidedly no," I said. "There's a nice coffee shop just down Chestnut Street where they let you sit out with your dog."

Nathaniel started off with Cyrus in the opposite direction. "I don't put caffeine or alcohol in my body," he said.

Bloody glad to hear it, I thought. Carrie non-suits such prissy renunciations, and puts her virtue where it counts...

I turned to find her quietly sobbing. Directly I enveloped her in my arms.

"Hell gnaw his bones! I will be hanged if some busy and insinuating rogue -- "

"It's not Nathaniel," she said.

"What?" I said. "Then who?"

"It isn't anyone, it's *everything!*" Carrie bawled. "And I'm getting pretty sick of crying. That's not me at all!"

It wasn't. "You need a good fighting campaign, love. Not you for fatted peace and lovey-dovey."

"I don't know," she said, squeezing my hand. "I'd take a little of that, if I could have it how I want it."

I felt shamed. No gentleman...

"Nathaniel yodeling outside, Mother haunting your bedside drinking her Third. It outpasses Poe," I said. "Did she scare you?"

"No, she calmed me. I was crying when she appeared."

"Over what, if Nathaniel's such a harmless hobbledehoy?"

She pressed her head against my chest. "I was... hating Deborah."

"Ah."

"And suddenly your mother was there, and she never touched me, but I felt caressed somehow, and she said, 'All things shall be well.'"

"Iago said that. It means everyone dies and goes screaming to hell."

"Actually," Carrie said, "I believed her, and fell into a beautiful sleep. Then I woke up this morning and nothing's better."

I kissed her. "Who says? Nathaniel sodded off. We're in each other's arms. As for Deborah -- "

Carrie pulled back and looked into my eyes. "Yes? What about her?"

I looked off because I couldn't hold her gaze. "Sorry, love. Someday I'll learn to put the good news last. With Deborah it's no news, and sadly in our case that's not the same as good."

SOME NEWS

The new school week came as a relief. I could banish the ghosts awhile. It was almost better for once to have Grime Bat and Blow Torch rather than Carrie in the faculty room with me. Easy to say this time, since the monsters of the deep were anyway engrossed in dissecting the previous night's "Sopranos."

Then there was Larry.

"'ello, 'ello," I muttered, as I sat down with my coffee.

"Ditsabouta time youza here," my tech pal said.

I blinked. "Beg pardon? What is it I didn't catch there?"

Larry looked at me loopily, eyes bloodshot and unfocused. "Zup? Zu late, dzude. Z'all." He turned to his own coffee, shakily tearing open a wad of sugar packets and dumping them all into his mug.

"Is this some ill-rehearsed performance," I said, "or have you actually gone dotty crackers?"

Larry hoovered down half his mug. "*Ahhhza!*" he exhaled with satisfaction, and smacked his lips. "Ahmina luvvina life, dzude."

Right. I judged I'd now been given something to go on. "You be-bopping baboon, you're not fit to address decent folk or even students."

Larry shrugged this off without looking at me. "Zzgool. Nemworryaboutit."

"Ah, good then." I tossed a glance at Blow Torch and Grime Bat who paid us no mind. "Step into the hall a minute. I have something you'll need to hear."

We stepped out, Larry first, me shutting the door behind us. No children or staff appeared.

"Zokay," Larry said, turning to me. "Whatsagot?"

"Only this," I said, and cracked my open hand smartly across his cheek and jaw.

"*Ow!* Jeevis bashevis! You said you had something to tell me!"

"I said I had for you something to hear. I perfectly heard my hand smiting your face. Didn't you?"

Larry touched his reddening cheek. "But what for?"

I placed a hand on my blinking friend's shoulder. "It's clear you're powerless in this. Thirty years' crushing repression can't be released in a weekend without insanity breaking out."

Larry seemed still waking from the daft sort of dream visited upon all of us. "Huh?"

"Let's not spend precious time being coy," I said. "It's sound thinking that's wanted now, as the repercussions could be heavy and far-reaching."

"Wha -- ?"

I ticked off points with my fingers. "Certes, you'll need to get working on transfer plans, preferably outside the district. You'll want to be unfailingly gallant and correct whilst maintaining an unbreakable chastity, avoiding at all costs her black widow's boudoir of doom."

"Who?"

"Understand she'll not sleep," I went on. "In this your quite unspeakable mutual madness you are the lamb and she the wolf. So it's best you proceed with all sober dispatch or I shall be sad to stand in short order at yet another grave."

Larry was by now thrown back again into the jumpy idiocy of minutes before. "Dude, what're ya talkin' about? I said life'sa good."

I now seized rather than patted his shoulder, pressing a thumb against the collar bone.

"Are you gonna slap me again?"

"No," I said, releasing him. "Slapping around loved ones is like reading bad books, deleterious to the character."

From around the hallway corner came a portentous humming, of an old disco tune. Larry and I froze looking at each other. The soft humming voice elevated to its familiar alto-tenor.

"Gentlemen," said Fay Muck. She stood in front of us but addressed me. "Can I borrow Mr. Berkowitz for a minute?"

Larry stood twitching like a dart-shot tuna.

"Ye little think how nigh your change approaches," I whispered.

"Huh?" Larry said.

"Read your Milton."

"Come on, snap it up," Fay Muck said.

...when all these delights will vanish and deliver ye to woe...

"I have an Uncle Milton," Larry said.

"So long, old man," I said.

Larry walked behind La Muck down the hall toward her office.

More woe, the more your taste is now of joy...

I performed a dead march back to the faculty room.

"What gives?" said Blow Torch, with the instinct of one who doesn't miss much. "What'd you do with the poor schnook?"

I sat heavily. Mad apparitions of the days and nights fled through me.

"There's nothing can be done with him, to him, for him," I said. "Nothing now. He's rhymed the Muck – without benefit of tenure!"

END BOOK TWO, PART ONE

THE CHESTERFIELD HOURS

Part Two

MUCK AND MIRE

Everybody's doing it. With such easy justification, there goes Empire, or what's left of it.

I wasn't doing it. Perhaps redressing the new Sodom was up to me.

Carrie Hahn needed a fighting campaign, and she wasn't doing it either.

True, the passionate intensity of abstinence can go very wrong indeed. Witness what "the worst" around the globe have gotten up to, on deciding that if they can't shag no other bloke shall. The good onward-type Anglican soldier, Churchill or Chesterfield, isn't having *that* slouch toward Bethlehem.

But look to the other end of it. If those who are "at it" include the Hoepplewhites, the Deborahs, the Mucks, and any rum barrelful of Hollywood strumpets, then the principled celibate are put in a two-front war. Where the bloody hell to start?

I put it to Carrie directly. "Look, we've got to pull Berkowitz out of the mire, before Muck's got him reamed, steamed, and buried out back with every dead Yorkie she's ever put a mu-mu on."

"But your family – "

"Won't abate in their own tawdry mischief long enough to let me tend to Larry!"

"If you'd let me finish," Carrie said, "I was going to say your family crisis comes first. Larry actually seems pretty happy."

I let that nauseating idea die in the air. "Let's assume my mother to be conventionally dead. Though it seems offish to me."

"And to me," my love replied, "not believing in ghosts."

"Nevertheless," I said, waving a days-old newspaper, "I choose to accept the official account."

A large headline read, *Heiress Feared Lost on Riviera*. The sub-head read *Madcap Dive off Industrialist's Yacht Proves Fatal*.

"Let me see that," Carrie said, snatching the paper from me. *"The Ffoulkes scion's host and reputed lover,"* she read, *"cabbage titan Baron Siegfried von Bourbognundvermuten, said only 'It cannot be. She lives as a budding green leaf forever.'"*

She lowered the paper and looked at me. "Oh poo," she said. "You're buying this?" We were in her classroom, blissfully alone for now.

"You ask whether I buy it as fact?" I said. "Or as poo? I tell you I accept it as written."

Carrie stood and moved close to me. We had, you know, a palpable inclination. Indeed, we seemed two likely puzzle pieces begging for an almighty but distracted Player simply to fit us.

"Then there's your father," she said. "And always there's Deborah."

"Then there's your spaniel Nathaniel," I countered, pulling her a final inch to me.

"Then there's The Fortune," she said, cinching me at the hips.

Glib facility deserted me at this. The removal of two Ffoulkes generations in two weeks' time, with the second shoe dropping so dubiously, had not come fully home to me. I broke from Carrie's embrace.

"There is no Fortune," I said, and fled the room.

Right. It was Berkowitz who needed attention. Daphne Ffoulkes Chesterfield's ghostly midnight visits had short-circuited grief. If those feelings would not come, then I would not, like some cheap vaudevillian, lachrymosely call them up. First things first…

"I mean, should I just dash your brains out now on the porcelain unit of the little boys' room?"

"Uh, no," Larry said. We were alone in the tech lab.

"It would do you a mercy," I said, "and research labs'll want to sift through the brains that work world-wide magic on a computer yet can't keep your pizzle out of our boss."

"Actually," Larry said in a sort of awed whisper, "she's kinda hot. You should see her in Victoria's Secret."

"Good God!"

"I know it's risky, but I can't help myself. I go around singing all the time."

"Right," I said. "You hear her name, and you're aflame."

"She's not a fox, she's a *cougar*."

I held my guts, puffed my cheeks, and generally made a show of keeping my oatmeal down.

"Bleah! Wonder where you got that one. A trendy self-appellation that originates with the first outbreak of spider veins."

Larry pulled up to his full five-foot eight, and jutted his chin out. "Take that back or you're a dead man."

In response I took a negligent stance and looked away out the window.

"You've fared so well in combat against Chesterfields," I said. "One fake knockout achieved, one real knockout absorbed."

Larry may have read somewhere that tough guys ball their fists, bounce on the balls of their feet, and just get all over bally. He made a passing show of it.

Suppressing a giggle, I eased toward the door, which opened inward and bashed me in the face, spinning me in a tarantella against the wall.

The petite figure of Carrie Hahn appeared. "What are you *doing*?" she said.

I regarded her through the web of my fingers. "Just breaking yon door over the bridge of my nose, love. But it's nothing."

"Well, here's something." She turned to Larry, who had unballed himself and stood gaping at her.

"Our tenure reviews are set for the week after next. Mine's got Fay and some board members visiting in and out from Monday to Wednesday. Yours is with just Fay on that Friday."

Larry, who seemed to grasp only now the relation of cougar to prey, paled round the gills and sank heavily into the swivel chair by his main computer.

"Ah, good then," said I, who had nailed down tenure in the pre-Muck days of Arden. "You'll be sure to bring your A game that day, eh what, old man? And the night before?"

With my class due back from gym, I left the two hopefuls to their thoughts and prospects.

EGGS AND BANGERS

I'd long trained myself not to play at things that brought me no advantage. And there was no advantage to driving past Carrie Hahn's flat whilst she was out. In fact it was not a gentlemanly thing to do, and not by way of giving one a virtuous feeling.

But the persistent sense that things are offish can lead to offish acts. I surrendered to temptation. Upon the porch, sitting in a chair and reading, was the lad Nathaniel. Perhaps Cyrus sat out of sight at his feet. Did the blighter have a key? Did he hang like a bat from the rafters every night? Was this a worthy thing for me to dwell upon?

Don't dwell then, rather turn things round a bit. I never looked back in the mirror as I left Carrie's behind me. I was already thinking that I must go with her sometime soon to her homestead in the Finger Lakes, perhaps to celebrate her tenure. She at least must have a sane parent or even two, of whatever heritage, and it was time, it was time, to prepare a face for the people that you meet. That is to say, for proper introductions.

I might view it as proper, but would the senior Hahns? It was harder and harder to remember myself a married man, but the father of a marriageable maiden would not be forgetting it. Compared to some presumed lascivious geezer with a wife in the woodpile, Nathaniel might seem viable timber.

But a gentleman does not, as the psychobabblers say, catastrophize. Nor does he allow for the possibility that his honourable intentions should

123

be questioned. We would go, we would go to the Lakes… if Carrie wished it.

Now it was time to drop in on an actual lascivious geezer, with a wife not in the woodpile, instead somewhere between the devil and the deep blue sea.

"Well," Captain Jack Chesterfield said, letting in me his son, "it's just like old times."

As it was Sunday morning, I had dog Daisy with me, and we went straight to the kitchen as in Sunday brunch days of yore.

"Except that it's nothing like," I said, coming face to face with Deborah sitting at the table behind omelet and coffee.

"Daisy, sweetheart!" Deborah said, dropping her fork with a clank and reaching a hand out. Daisy merely sat by my side.

"Old woman, she knows ye not," I said. "Or perhaps she does."

"You jerk, you've brainwashed her!"

"Twaddle," I said. "Daisy is a lady. She cuts you of her own good breeding."

"Come on now," my guv'nor said as he joined us. "We're all Christians here."

"Are we?" I said. "I thought maybe I was Dr. Livingstone amongst the pagans. Those are pretty barbarous-looking omelets compared to what Mother made."

"Oh right," Jack said, with a bow of the head. "It's a sad time for us all, another reason not to bicker."

"Well, we're not Italians," I said, "so I don't ask we perform opera over Mother. Still, it's a bit *sang froid* even for us Frozen Chosen. And a bit thick."

124

"My dear," Deborah said, "it isn't real to us, Daphne being gone. How could it be?"

"Ah. I was just thinking the same about this little *ménage* of yours. How indeed could it be?"

Jack only grunted. Deborah shifted tack.

"I so wanted to speak my little piece at Granny's service. Just for you and Daphne, I had my Shakespeare ready: 'We that are young shall never see so much, nor live so long.'"

"Sorry," I said, "you only get to say that if like Edgar you've slain an evil bastard. Begetting one won't qualify, if you're wondering."

"Have some eggs, will you," Jack said. "Sit, sit."

I sat. Daisy lay herself down beneath the table.

A fat envelope bearing some law firm's letterhead rested on the counter. I merely glimpsed it before I sat to table. What in all this murkily disreputable, even supernatural chain of events could produce even a dreary sort of "closure"? There was no knowing...

I half rose again, like a tradesman invited to the Quality's table, who shoots his cuffs in self-conscious dignity. Another glance at the law envelope revealed some wiggly lines and a *Par Avion* stamp. A sneaking-on, cat-footed feeling of wicked joy came over me.

"Pretty good eggs, Dad," I said, brightening. "Aesthetics be damned."

"I always said damn aesthetics," Jack said. "And always I'd be one against two." Again he remembered late to bow his old gray head for Daphne.

Deborah sent by the Captain a pea-shot of the armor-piercing scorn she could fire on a man falling short of scratch. Benedict Hoepplewhite had caught the howitzer load.

"You would damn aesthetics?" she asked Jack. "With me in the room?"

With you in the bed, I thought. But instead I chuckled and sunnily said:

"It should kill me to say this, but you two are a couple in a million."

Deborah, still with half a mad on, turned to me warily. "What?"

I shrugged. "It's palpable. I guess in a way I'm looking from outside now. But really I've never seen such a rare pair for companionability, for at-homeness, for chemistry if I must gorge the word up."

The guv'nor looked down at his eggs. Deborah chewed over, rather than swallowed the bait.

"You just want to marry that little sparrow," she said.

"Guilty as charged," I said.

"And boink her, with sanction of clergy, since you won't get with the twentieth century, much less the twenty-first."

Defensiveness now would be death. "If ever spliced, we will assuredly boink," I said. "But I'd marry her even if I were Lord Chatterley."

"Hm." Deborah glanced at Jack, half-tenderly this time, and put a hand on his.

The Captain would no sooner bawl out love oaths than surrender his sidearm to Ho Chi Minh. Thus the sight of Jack's big paw enveloping Deborah's slender manicured fingers was, to my rejoicing, a gaudy balcony scene.

126

One doesn't overstay.

"Right," I said. "Must get on now. Thanks again. Come, Daisy."

As I piled with Daisy into the car, I recurred to my high school days, and the mantra of the old college application game: Fat Envelopes Good.

THE CHESTERFIELD HOURS

HAPPINESS IS THIS... OR THAT

There was a fair bit of Sunday still left. What does one say of the humble domestic chores that necessarily fill such hours? I, it is to be remembered, had a house and grounds to maintain. My love Carrie Hahn had her own flat, with a bumptious Labrador adding to the maintenance load. A full school week lay out before us as well. The reader who finds in these realities some fatal narrative slack is invited to go purchase the software that will iron it out for us.

Anyway, raking, mowing, clean-up, dressing, marketing, dog-walking, cooking, dinner, class-prep and dishwashing brought bedtime timely round, with me properly feeling "a good tired." One sleeps like the blessed dead...

Tinkle-inkle...

"My brilliant boy."

I sat up in bed. "Mother?"

"Who else? Blimey, dear, how you've foxed them!"

I located a wavering form, again bluish in the moon-dappled dark near the window. Ice again tinkled and stirred. "Since when am I so brilliant?" I said.

"I always said so," Daphne said.

"You never said so. It's what mothers of stupid boys say." Daisy, as on the last visitation, sat still by my feet, staring rapt at the figure by the window.

The ice tinkled an instant, then went silent, immersed as Daphne tippled. Her family ring glinted in the moonlight.

"That's probably true," she said. "But no stupid boy could play it out so neatly after one glimpse of Swifty's letter."

"Whose?"

Daphne chuckled softly. "Swifty Treves-Alsace, our solicitor across the pond. So you don't deny what you saw, or the devilish clever way you played it."

"Pretty elementary, I thought. It came from Europe to say you're dead. But aren't these things supposed to take seven years or something?"

"Not anymore, dear. You'll recall that billionaire balloonist that blew away to hell? Already declared dead. His ought to be a warmish probate."

"But give Dad some credit, Mother. He's not doing a celebratory dance as Deborah seems wanting to."

"She won't dance till they're married," Daphne said. "You certainly gave that a push today, my Sherlock." She tipped and drank again.

"Well, if you're happy, and they're happy together, I'll certainly be happy for Carrie and me to get on with it. There is no Fortune, of course."

Daphne chuckled again. "Well, there'd jolly well better be, or they jolly well *won't* be happy. Or Deborah won't be, and won't be giving him that horizontal happiness he prizes above wealth."

I had come from deep slumber, and it began to pull at me once more.

"The horizontal's her only currency," I said, and yawned.

"Till it leverages purchase of the other."

I, who hated filthy lucre and only wanted nine bean rows with Carrie, Daisy and Cyrus, felt weariness wash over me. I fell back onto my pillow.

"Well, happiness to their sheets," I said, and closed my eyes.

"I think not, dear," she seemed to say, the voice subsiding to a dying fall.

THE CHESTERFIELD HOURS

BUMPED

In our daily movements, we are brushed by cultural blight we'd prefer not to acknowledge. The gentleman or lady may be hard-trained not to react, but he or she will notice it.

The supermarket is, by its nature, "of the people." So the gentleman gets in and gets out, rather than linger in its bedlam sensibility.

But his gaze will not miss the tabloids. He will not buy them, they task him, but they are always there. He knows that Celebrity Cellulite must sell copies, or it would not be updated literally *ad nauseam*.

If the gentleman is myself, and insists on knowing directly all insidious threats to the nation's soul, he will even know what The Bump is. At the tabloid rack, Bump issues are snapped up by proletariettes with "bump issues" already, given them by fellows known only, like the Sacred Soldier, to God, and maybe the police.

Of course no decent narrative treats of such subjects...

"Oh, my Gooawd!" Blow Torch Borch screeched in the faculty room. "The harrar! The harrar!"

"The bump! The bump!" chorused Grime Bat Grimmboat.

Fay Muck had only just left the room. I, seated at the long table's other end, played it dumb and silent.

"You two are terrible," Carrie Hahn said to the cackling hens. "Fay's forty-two, I think. She's entitled to have a little stomach."

Blow Torch snorted indulgently. "You're such a dolling child. Really you're too precious."

"Scrape the scales off your eyes, Carrie dear," Grime Bat said. "Fay's a maniac for dieting and the gym. One pound gained and it's a thousand crunches a day and rice cakes for a month."

Larry Berkowitz walked in. I softly cleared my throat – a head's up, you know.

"Ah then!" I said, to turn the page. "What news on the tenure front? We've not talked lately."

The Memorial Day break had passed, four days instead of three because of unused snow days, and with Daphne Ffoulkes Chesterfield's visitation and assorted distractions, it had felt like a sabbatical.

Larry looked preoccupied. He also sported a bruise about his eye and cheekbone. "Oh," he said. "Tenure's Friday."

I stood. "Right. Let's go chat about it."

Out in the hall, Larry turned jumpy as a cat. "Are you going to belt me like the last time you pulled me out here?"

I gently touched his eye. "You've *been* belted. Now we've got to stop you getting mugged on Friday."

"Huh?"

"What's the time and temperature with you and your... paramour?"

"Like, Fay?"

I looked to the ceiling, spread out my upturned hands and crooked my fingers hungrily for the straight skinny.

"Yes, right, the little mother."

"The what?"

I seized Larry with both hands by the shirt collar.

"I lied," I said. "You've not been belted yet, not properly."

The hallway, providentially, was empty. Then the faculty door squeaked.

"What is it with you boys?" Carrie Hahn said. "You're stupid all the time."

I unhanded Larry. "One of us is," I said. "The technical genius who doesn't know what comes from the first thing in the world."

Larry implored Carrie, "Will you tell him to make sense? I'm sick of English talk."

"You haven't tried it," I said.

Carrie took each of us by an arm. "My room now," she said. "We have ten minutes."

To show us the boss she first sat us both in kindergarten chairs. I splayed my longish legs out. Larry fit a little better. Carrie stood over us both.

"Before we get to the rest of it," she said, addressing me, "did you beat him up?"

I looked off insolently, like Sam Spade with the coppers. "Of course not. Muck did."

"She didn't beat me up!" Larry said indignantly.

"All right then," Carrie said. "Next subject." She turned to Larry. "Who are your tenure session students?"

Larry didn't teach full classes. He did hour-long tech sessions with small groups. On one of these, Friday, hung his future.

"Prudence Piotrowski," he said.

"Okay."

"Angola Pitts-Noire."

"Fine."

"And... Dylan Czarnecki."

"Oh."

"Rotten luck, old man," I said. "They couldn't give you Satan or bin Laden?"

"He hasn't been so bad," Larry said. "We talk. He likes Grand Theft Auto, and so do I."

"To you it's a game. To him it's a training exercise for Friday's session."

Larry involuntarily tensed. Carrie stepped in.

"Stop it," she said. "You're going to make him nervous, needlessly."

I shifted things. "Well, yours is underway, eh love? How'd this morning go?"

"Oh, a breeze," Carrie said. "They stopped in first thing, saw me get them settled in and started. They stayed a half hour and said 'see you tomorrow.' Very cheerful."

"No doubt." I shifted once more, turning grimly to Larry.

"So how long we going to ignore the eight-hundred-pound stork in the room?"

Carrie gave a little gasp. Larry reddened. The hall bell rang.

There was time, a minute at least, to address it before we went to our students again. But Larry was off, like a missile. I stood in Carrie's doorway.

"You're not, as they say, in denial?" I asked her.

Her hands were to her face. "Can I know in my heart it's true, and still deny it?"

"No. It's got to be faced out. And there's no talking to the dumb sap, so it's up to us to save Friday for him."

The halls had filled. Students and teachers flowed by.

Carrie, with kindergarteners, had to fetch them personally each time.

"It's getting to be so much more than Friday," she said as she took up her bag.

I was edging away. "For now there's nothing else. It's Dunkirk, love. If Friday goes wrong, the whole game's up!"

SEE ME

Right. Carrie and I might be small ships, but Larry was a rubber ducky caught between the blitzkrieging Muck and the treacherous Channel. In that Channel was a savage little ankle-biter named Czarnecki, who must be dealt with. That's what pals are for.

As I hustled back to class, Fay Muck floated up, said "See me" and passed by.

Well, I was in class the rest of the afternoon, so I had time to reflect. What the devil could she want of me? One must remember, when summoned before authority, one's own strengths. I was tenured and, I believed, valuable. As a male elementary teacher who delivered year after year sterling results, I was something of a hot-stuff wonder: in effect, quota hire and top producer in one package. That was spine-stiffening.

And I had met Fay Muck's husband, upon his ejection from her office during Super Bowl week. That suddenly struck me, I knew not why, as functional intelligence. The pathetic sod that week had the Eagles to win, perhaps one reason he hadn't been seen since.

Fay Muck might be another reason, and a bigger... but there was no knowing...

Dylan Czarnecki had grown perhaps two inches and packed on fifteen pounds since I doused him with Carrie Hahn's soup in the late winter.

This menacing fact further affirmed my own worth. A bold and fit six-footer who'll none of it is a bulwark against hooligan anarchy. And it was sadly ironic that Larry Berkowitz, having Dylan only one hour per week, could as a consequence be a Starbucks barrista this time next year.

So before checking in with Muck, I sidled up like a spider to the fly in the ointment.

"I say, Czarnecki," I said. "Do you know what Friday is?"

Dylan wiped his mouth, still stained from lunch. "Day of the week?"

"Ah, good. You're scoring now at kindergarten level." Such sarcasm represents child abuse in some precincts today -- but, sorry, no pity towards any villain when a pal's in peril.

"I'm asking if you know what's happening Friday that's out of the usual," I said as ominously as I could.

This Czarnecki possessed some primitive wiliness of his own. "Sure," he said, "Fay's coming to watch geek-face Berkowitz teach me 'n my two computer ho's."

Whom does the gentleman defend first here?

"Mark this, Czarnecki," I said, "and mark it for your life and health. When *Doctor* Muck comes to observe *Mister* Berkowitz teaching you and the young *Misses* Piotrowski and Pitts-Noire, you will be at all times a gentleman. Else you'll answer to me."

The dismissal bell rang.

Dylan lurched to his feet, and his hundred and sixty pounds sent the desk skidding. "You can't do s--- to me now," he said. "Me and Fay are tight, and Berkowitz's a— is grass." And, as he never brought homework, he shambled as lightly away as any unencumbered orangutan would do.

With the school day done, I went on to Fay Muck's office. As I walked, I ruthlessly analyzed whether a true crisis even existed. Mightn't the Muck, mired in turpitude, naturally tenure Larry, who was anyway deserving, with the least fuss necessary? And wouldn't Czarnecki, whose Friday afternoon default mode was a bored surliness, want to simply get the dismal session, and the week, over with?

Yet I couldn't rest easy…

"Me and Fay are tight," the leering brat had said.

???!!!

Shadows fled across the translucent glass of the window reading *Dr. Fay Muck, Building Principal*, and the crazy remembrance of all that Super Bowl week Muck-chucking, of Le by La, fled likewise through me now.

The curvy female shadow (*avec* bump!) bent over a seated, cowering male one.

I had my hand up to knock. Barging right in, after a quick rap, might yield actionable intelligence...

"What a grob!" Fay Muck's voice hissed. "Three weeks and you're history."

Something – oh, call it Provvy – pulled my hand back.

Instead of barging, I turned on my heel and walked away. I wouldn't "see" Fay Muck today. Only with Carrie would I see it through for friend Larry.

DEMON LOVERS

I've mentioned that weeknights are not party nights, for the Chesterfield-and-Carrie sort of chaste hard-working lovers. Dogs must be seen to. Always there are errands, and then there is class prep. Dinner fits in where it will.

There is of course the telephone. Granted, many people in severing the old land-line have severed themselves from common courtesy and filled our world with blather.

But a gentleman uses the phone not to annoy strangers, but for the nurture and renewal of his loving relations. This is best accomplished by calling when the loved one is most "at home." For Carrie Hahn, that was tennish...

"Hello?"

"Evening, love. Wishing you a good sleep before Muck and company visit again in the morn."

"Oh, thanks. I'm sure it'll be fine."

"Never a doubt."

"Quite," she said crisply, to tickle me, and it did.

Couldn't resist this one: "Nathaniel about?"

She took a small breath, nothing gaspish. "Well, I fed him something earlier, then put him out."

"Still your spaniel," I said. Jealousy, if it had ever existed, had dissolved.

"He can fend," Carrie said. "He doesn't have to go home, but he can't stay here. And he's stopped singing."

"Perhaps he sings to another bird now."

"As if," my love said. "But he's welcome to."

A gentleman can kill two birds whilst nurturing the true love – and Provvy seemed nudging me to venture it.

"Gosh," I said, "but I'd like to see your old lake country home sometime. Shall we, once school's over and your tenure's in hand?"

"Might just be done," she said. "It would help if you were separated at least."

"Ah."

"As you hinted might actually happen."

"Yes, Deborah seems to have had an epiphany of sorts. But she's a baffler."

"Well," Carrie said, "you and Daisy would love the Lakes. And Father would certainly get a kick out of meeting and contesting with you."

A third bird was flushed into the air. Take dead aim...

"Would you in any sense see Larry Berkowitz as a grob, love?"

"Excuse me?"

"Deuced unflattering term, grob. Not our Larry, surely?"

Carrie giggled. "Well, it's funny-sounding anyway," she said. "Got to be Yiddish. But I haven't a clue."

A clean miss. Let it pass...

"Well," I said, "I fear our pal's in trouble. But we can't map a campaign tonight."

"No."

"And you've got your own to worry about. Forgive me, love."

"Not at all. I agree we've got to see to Larry."

I let out a sigh of relief. "So glad to hear you say that. Then we'll have more of this tomorrow."

We rang off. Good at least to have Carrie with her own tenure near at hand, so we could focus on the stickier Larry wicket.

But something was dicky. That Carrie didn't know who or what a grob was, I accepted implicitly. But thanks to an improving book titled "The Joys of Yiddish" by Leo Rosten, I knew what a grob was, and wasn't.

Larry Berkowitz might be a shlemiel, a shmendrick... might even be, sexually, a shnorrer. But Larry Berkowitz was no grob – and Fay Muck, if she could use the term, must know the distinctions.

I took the dickiness into an uneasy sleep...

Tink...

Thus at the first icy note I sat up.

"Mother, can it keep? It's a rugged week for me, and only just begun."

Came a heavy clinking, and giggling – a strange unison sort of giggling. "Darling boy, you don't want to miss this visit. You've been positively calling it up!"

Focus took hold, as I peered toward the bluish shape by the window. But there seemed more fullness about Daphne Ffoulkes Chesterfield this time: O menopausal madness! Not that!

Of course not that. There was another presence in the room.

"What ho, Mother. Who's the geezer?"

In fact it was a man younger than Daphne, though older than myself. He held a full drink identical to hers, and wore a dark beret rakishly tilted nearly over one eye. And he was shadily familiar...

141

"Meet Siggy, darling," Daphne said. "My huckleberry friend."

"From the Riviera, purportedly," I said. "Sharing your taste for bourbogne und vermuten."

"Hee-hee-hee!" the ghostly pair said in chorus, and clinked glasses.

"I say, do cabbages have titans?" I said. "Mongers, maybe."

"Hee-hee-hee!"

"How," I asked, "can I have called up this abominable specter?" I squinted at the man, who was nothing of Fitzgerald's Riviera, or even Hitchcock's. Beret aside, he struck me as decidedly, disreputably local.

"Don't say abominable, dear," Daphne said. "You've had it down to Provvy all along, and Siggy and I fervently hope you're right."

"I know you now," I said, inwardly with a shiver.

"Nice to see ya again," the man said. "Sig Muck."

"So it's murder!"

The man turned to Daphne, and they clinked glasses again.

"As to that," Sig Muck said, "I can't tell you yes, but I won't say no."

"Hee-hee-hee!" they chortled as I swooned back into slumber.

END BOOK TWO, PART TWO

Part Three

TOO TERRIBLY TERRIBLE

On tenure week Tuesday, Carrie and I tried to have a strategy sit-down. The faculty room was unsafe, given the big ears of Blow Torch and Grime Bat. True security dictated a move to Carrie's room...

"Zounds!" I said as I just avoided tripping onto my face. "What's a bloody *tricycle* doing here now?"

"It's a long story," Carrie said, pushing it away with a casual flick of her foot. "Sit," she added.

"Where, on the trike? Probably better than your devilish little dormouse chairs."

"Where you will," she said, sitting down behind her desk.

"I will here then," I said, parking one haunch on the desk.

"Did you know," she said, "that Nathaniel is calling it a day?"

"Really," I said. "If only it weren't metaphor, as he's been at least a fortnight on our hands."

"If you and I were actually carrying on, he might filibuster till the end of time," she said. "But I think he's more convinced by... by the way we are."

"Ah. Well, there's a lesson there – for whom, I've no idea."

"It's also," she said, "the kind of thing that impresses Father."

"Mm. He and Nathaniel are on the page together, eh?"

"Oh no. Nathaniel is just a boy to him."

"Ah then. Poppa and I are together on *that* page." The Berkowitz tenure file must presently be re-opened, but I didn't like damming up this new flowage.

"Listen," Carrie said. "You and Larry are invited up for the weekend after school ends. You'll share a nice room over the stables."

Stables! So chat has no purpose?

"Super," I said. "I shall be honored."

"And you must bring Daisy, of course."

"She'll be likewise honored."

The bell rang. "We haven't gotten to Larry!" she said.

"Must we?" I said, really quite excited about the invitation. "He can job-hunt in the Lakes as easily as here."

"Don't be terrible," she said. "We'll save him yet."

The halls were filling. I got up to go.

"D'you think he'd actually go with us up to your folks'?"

"Of course not," she said, her green eyes ingenuously wide. "He's totally the beard. Mother and Father would never invite you alone."

"Now who's terrible?" I said as I slipped away. Smashing girl, I thought as I plunged through the roiling halls to my room.

WEDNESDAY

So that was a chance chucked away – for Larry's tenure, that is. I wasn't sure I anymore cared. My own affairs were shaping up nicely as summer break approached. For it promised a break of another sort, in the untidy stand-off that was my marriage. With Captain Jack and Deborah cooing and counting their chickens, and with the Hahns' invitation, things were looking up. Perhaps the Berkowitzes, Mucks, and Czarneckis should be left to their own grotty dealings.

But no. Wednesday found Carrie Hahn pretty warm for action. Something, somehow, had settled over her. This time she found me in my own empty room, with both our classes at lunch.

"All right," she said. "Let's get cracking, and not waste any more time."

"Let's, dear," I said, with a sweep of an arm. "Take any old sixth-grade chair you please."

"Don't be a snot about my room," she said.

"Plotz," I said.

Again no reaction to the yiddishism – but she did sit.

"I was only just thinking," I said, "that maybe we should step back and let it unfold in all its appalling deviancy. Just like modern life."

"And I'm only now thinking," Carrie replied, "that you're perfectly wrong. It must be blown up completely and postponed till it can be done by people of integrity."

"You're a filly with a hotfoot. What's it all about?"

She took a deep breath and blew it out. "I'm not letting Fay just run amok. She's out of control!"

It dawned belatedly on me, occupied as I'd been all morning, that Carrie's own tenure review was now completed.

"Did she and her gang give you a bad time this morning?" I asked.

"Oh no. Everything swam along." She added almost tearfully, "I'm sure I'm a cinch!"

"Well then, as she and Larry have made their bed, should we not let them go on happily to hell together?"

She was not actually going to cry. She devoured my eyes with her own – penetratingly. "You're being Socratic," she said. "You don't mean that."

I met her gaze without flinching. "I don't, of course. But he's young enough to recover."

"How about this, then," she said. "Fay was flat as a board this morning!"

Signifying, you know, more than an eighth-grade lassie unstuffing the trainer. "Below stairs?" I near to gasped.

She faintly nodded, but with a fierce look.

"So," I said grimly, "the Bump has gone off to join her heart, someplace long ago and far away."

"I'm not having her deciding Larry's fate," Carrie said. "I don't care what it takes."

"I've just had two rummy thoughts, love," I said.

"Oh?"

"Yes, I overheard something outside Muck's office that tells me Larry's DOA already."

She quite had her jaw set now. "I propose all-out intervention, up to and including a commando raid. What's rummy thought two?"

"Just this. In our recent campaigns, we've supplied the boldness, of which Larry has none. But he's supplied the technical genius. Where do we go for that now?"

The passing bell was imminent. Carrie glanced at the clock and rose.

"Go nowhere but to me," she said. "I'm smuggling a wire into that room Friday."

"Brilliant girl! The lives of others, and all that."

The bell rang.

"And," she said, "Nathaniel will make himself useful before he leaves town."

This time it was she who slipped out into the burgeoning halls, as I sat and pondered.

R & S

Much as I treasured my fleeting moments with Carrie Hahn, I felt done with strategizing. We would do our best for a pal, and then let the chips fall. I well remembered my Lucky Jim where the hero frets the college term away, obsessed with the preservation of his miserable instructor's job. He attends manfully to an awful boss and an hysterical girlfriend, only to get the sack from the former, and the mitten from the latter. Yet when it all sorts out he's got a better job and a better girlfriend.

I of all people could not construct the future. And I felt a little "out of it" as concerned the Friday tenure session. Carrie was ready to jump all in – perhaps it was best left to her.

So for Thursday, something fresh was called for – something out of the building, something of my own. Friend Larry needed more than tenure. Nothing had come of Lucky Jim Dixon till he grew a spine and risked it -- and, admittedly, got drunk. And I had brooded on Larry's now-yellowing bruises...

"All right, you man," I said, taking Larry by the arm at the final bell Thursday. "You're coming with me. I only want an hour of your useless Play Station and Snackin' Cakes time."

We drove into that part of the metropolis with Italian bakeries, furniture warehouses – and the gymnasium Ripped & Shredded. As I parked on the street out front, I told Larry, "Your punching bag days are over."

I knew the kind of strong hands Larry needed now. Someone he'd physically have to respect, of the no-nonsense sergeant-major sort. Someone who would stiffen the Berkowitz spine, or snap it...

"I know you! How'd I ever miss trainin' you, and who's your little friend?"

"Right ho! It's Jeanine, is it not?"

All rippling tanned muscle beneath the platinum blonde locks, she bounded up to us with a dazzling smile, blue gum flashing like a sapphire in pearls. I thought of Carrie's Labrador Cyrus, another powerful, golden, good-humoured athlete.

"That is so correct!" she said. "And you are... cha cha... chooch... "

"Right, Chesterfield's the name. And this is -- "

"Deborah's husband! It's all comin' back to me now."

"Ahhhh... rrrright." It wouldn't do to likewise bring up B. Hoepplewhite just now.

"This is my pal, Larry Berkowitz. He needs a spine... er, he needs a good regimen, you know."

Larry stood goggling at this winsome Amazon. How she rated with his pantheon of two-dimensional graphic-novel goddesses, one could only guess. Pretty strongly, was my surmise, as Larry looked like fainting.

"Oh, man," Jeanine said, "what I can do for him. C'mere, ya little dickens." She grasped Larry by his thinnish shoulders, like an amorous linebacker. "Oh yeah!" she said. "Oh yeah, we can do some business here!"

If their business were a sort of tango – and who knew? – then Larry would be the one bent backward over Jeanine's knee, his rose in her teeth. And he might like it, very much.

One does not pump away at the good old bellows once the fire has caught, which is only to stress yet again that one doesn't overstay. "Well then," I said. "I'll leave you to it."

And I did, not that Larry noticed.

THE CHESTERFIELD HOURS

ALL A BIG NOTHING

That Thursday night came a call I'd been expecting, yet had not fully prepared myself for.

"I've decided," Deborah said, "to give you what you so clearly want. I think it can be done quite fast and cheaply if we approach it with civility."

Neither believing in nor desiring The Fortune, I might have let pass this sanctimonious *noblesse.* If the price to be with my true love was letting in Deborah to queen it about as America's first Lady Chesterfield, well, it was a small one to pay. Yet "fast and cheaply" did rankle a bit...

"Can we talk in a couple weeks, dear? All the year-end stuff is upon me, and I'm getting out of town for two days just after."

"Don't think *I'm* in such a big hurry," she said.

"Of course not, dear. Two weeks, then."

"Don't look a gift horse in the mouth."

"Not a bit of it, dear. Bye."

***

All was racing to climax, I realized as I prepared for bed that night. The romantic hopes of so many, the profound shapings of professional destiny – could everyone come out whole and happy? It seemed doubtful. I found myself pensive, reflective, and just a bit blue.

When destinies cross over each other, when one must lose for another to gain, we then conceive villains to ward off grief. Without a clear enemy, the destruction of human hope is too sad for any words. I understand there are real villains in the world, but they, like Iago, conceive themselves...

I was thinking of Fay Muck, and not comfortably. I had, I must acknowledge, a lingering affection for her. She had been a worthy adversary, in an arena where no battle was about so very much, and nothing so very sad or vicious ever was meant to be. We were so very different, and that had made us affectionate foes – she must feel it too, I was sure. Yet I, whom the Muck had not bothered "seeing" since our hallway pass-by, was probably now the furthest person from her mind.

Carrie now hated her. I, who had even more damning intelligence -- if such can reliably be gleaned from a ghost -- found I could not. True, I did not like to think of The Bump, whence it came, whither it went. But Carrie's revulsion was of another order, and this might point to heritage, something I had sportingly trusted to clarify itself in natural course. I was not, by nature and acculturation, a relativist lad. A gentleman does... a gentleman (or lady) does not. Yet by Whom was I chosen as judge or jury of anything?

One might assume Fay Muck, by her dress, language, interests, and demeanor to be of the Reform denomination of her faith. This status is subject to trenchant and humourous commentary, alike by persons within and without the faith. Such spoofing commentary would center on a certain liberality in all things, but prominently on liberality of language, mores and the body. Such liberality, it must be mentioned, is not funny to all people.

It would, however, be a scream normally to me, whose own denomination, in another faith, was not beyond spoofing, as it devolved in the twenty-first century into a sort of hedonistic bohemianism for blue-bloods. But people getting hurt, fired, even slain is not funny to those Reform or Anglican gentlefolk who are not psychopaths.

It could hardly be coincidence that Jeanine was on my mind as well. What a very good sort she was, and how men had wronged her – men including myself. That I had done so unthinkingly, that it took a Benedict Hoepplewhite to barge through the door to perdition which I had only playfully cracked – that was no absolution.

True, Jeanine was a grown girl, had been only too ready to touch Hoepplewhite's sticky new veneer of wealth and prominence; and true, she never knew of my email gambit, that had gone wrong in a largeish way. But, in spite of my earnest atonement of Super Bowl Eve, on this eerie Tenure Eve I took to bed feeling there was work still to be done there…

**

Tink –

"Right, Mother, don't expect me to go all spooked and crawly tonight. I fully expected you." I sat up in bed.

Next I heard the glass, and ice, tip. "D'you think it's my intention to scare my own son? It's called a visit, dear."

Even without surprise I took time to focus.

"Are you alone?" I said.

"Hee-hee-hee!"

"I say, Muck, you weren't so bloody mirthful in life, as I recall it. What's it all about?"

Sig Muck had the hoarse voice one gets from long acquaintance with grain spirits and coffin nails. Such a fellow shouldn't have much to laugh about, and the titter thus had an extra grating quality.

153

He said, chuckling, "I wish the Powers That Be would let me get a C-note down tomorrow on your buddy's tenure. Fay's gonna gut him."

"Thanks for the good word," I said. "I positively cleaned up on the Super Bowl, going the other way from you."

Daphne stood again in the bluish moonlight by the window, her disreputable new shadow hanging by her other shoulder.

She said, "Well, I don't share Siggy's view of Larry's chances, dear. It's our only quarrel." Her old ring streamed pearls off the moon.

"Siggy's a real grob, you know," I said before I could have it back. It simply popped to mind and out. "Say, you didn't materialize in Fay's office the other afternoon, by any chance?"

"Hee-hee-hee! Musta been some other grob. But if I did, what the hell, she couldn't kill me twice!"

A grob was a disreputable, uncouth, unclean swine of a fellow – all things Sig Muck was and Larry Berkowitz was not.

"The Powers would never allow it, dear," Daphne said. "Siggy's on a pretty tight leash – mine."

"I don't believe she killed you at all, old man," I said. "What with drinking, smoking, and betting with the Mafia, you were doing brilliantly for yourself."

"Well," Muck said, "you can kill someone without actually murdering him. Get me?"

"No," I said. "Enlighten me."

The slack and pudgyish form in the shadows actually seemed to slump a bit.

"If it's just too dispiriting, Siggy dear," Daphne said, "don't go on. You're in a better place now, where there's no 'performance anxiety,' as I believe they call it."

"Oh, do go on by all means," I said. "This is getting good."

Sig Muck waved his drink hand like a Rat Packer as he explained.

"She's gotta have it all the time! I'm not a young man, or a fit one. We had a little reconciliation a couple months back, and she trapped me in the bedroom for a whole weekend. I finally dragged myself off like an old elephant -- "

"And snuffed it. Right. And Fay knows nothing of your fate."

Sig Muck snorted bitterly. "Or care!"

"You're not ratty with my pal Larry, I hope? He's got a rough enough passage without a sort of a grobby jealous ghost after him."

"That pisher?" Muck said with a different, contemptuous snort. "I can't be bothered. His fun ended a couple weeks ago anyway."

"What? You can't mean it. They just had a frightful dust-up. It's why I'm so worried."

"Don't ever worry, darling," Daphne said. "About anything. It's all a big nothing."

"Listen," Muck said. "You want the emmis, you want to save your pal a big shtunk, get into Fay's desk sometime. You love to snoop, dontcha? More I cannot say."

"Siggy's doing you a good turn, dear," Daphne said. "He'll need someone to restore his name for posterity."

"But how, Mother? He doesn't even qualify for the ash-heap of history."

"You always find a way, dear."

Daisy was on my chest and licking me. As if her slobber were pixie dust, I went all drowsy.

Love... to... snoop...

CLIMAXIPALOOZA

I woke up alert and invigorated. Of course I was only a bit player. It was Larry who needed to perform today and Carrie, not I, committed to rescue him if he flopped.

Speaking of... as I pulled from the driveway and drove down my street to the four-way, I had a dream-like vision, that of Carrie Hahn parked in her car with the lad Nathaniel and the dog Cyrus. Neither train, plane, bus nor subway embarked from Chesterfield Station, so my neighborhood was not on the route for bunging Nathaniel back home. But as in a dream I simply waved to them and drove on. Carrie had a key to my house but, being a lady, had never used it.

My mornings were solid teaching, and I never saw Carrie or Larry to speak to till lunch hour. But since the year's work was all but in the barn now, at least I'd have a moment to properly tune Dylan Czarnecki. After taking attendance I sidled up.

"So, good my lad, I know you'll have a smooth tech session this aft."

"Huh?" The hulking malefactor, who hardly fit his chair anymore, looked up blankly before his eyes hardened.

I did not repeat myself or clarify. I simply stared the young blackguard down till he blinked.

"We'll see," Czarnecki said finally. "Depends on my mood."

"Actually it doesn't," I said. "You may come to meeting with ADD, ADHD, low-glycemic, bi-polar, suicidal, a latch-key kid or nose out of joint, but you will act the gentleman all the same."

"Like s--- "

"No, that's your regular standard. Today you're going to elevate a bit."

Czarnecki looked down at his desk and smirked. "Fay likes me the way I am."

"It's Doctor Muck, and I doubt it."

"Doctor Muck to you, dude. Fay to me."

There were actually other students to think of. I turned away.

"You're on notice," was all I told the blighter.

***

I could swear Carrie avoided me come lunchtime, but on seeking I found her in her room, fiddling with some gear out of a Radio Shack bag.

"Youch!" I yelled as, scouring below for landmines, I bopped my head against a model airplane dangling from a light fixture.

"Be right with you," Carrie said. "Make yourself comfortable."

"Impossible," I said, holding myself erect and wary. "What d'you have there?"

"Oh, something," she said, not looking me in the eye.

"A walkie-talkie?" I said, reading the box peeking out of the bag. "I'd thought they were, as the saying goes, so last century. So Eisenhowerian, even."

She still didn't look at me, instead played with the thing in a fascination, like her less-evolved peers at their cell-camera-phone-corders. But she held only one piece of the pair.

"I see Walkie," I said. "But where's Talkie?"

Finally she looked at me. "Oh, somewhere," she said.

Don't push it, I thought. "Say, it was rather a surprise to see you on my street with The Man Who Came to Dinner. Sorry I couldn't stop."

"Oh," she said. "Nathaniel just wanted to say goodbye."

That smelled a floater right there, but I let it pass.

"He's gone, then?"

Clearly uncomfortable, she said, "No, tomorrow actually."

The bell rang. "Can you be back here at one?" she said. "I've got Larry's lab all miked up for listening."

So she had some use for me after all. I stole a fast kiss.

"Will do, love. By hook or crook." With my head on a swivel I made it safely out of her debris-laden lair.

***

With the overlapping of lunch hour mods, I shared only twenty minutes with Carrie but a full forty with Larry, of which half remained. Where was the poor fatted calf?

In the tech lab, of course. I judged he must be burrowed in there like a soldier in his foxhole.

"'ello 'ello," I said on entering. "How you holding up?"

If Carrie was tense today, then Larry should be rubber room-ready. But he walked up with bright eyes and a smile.

"Great! Sore as hell, though."

"Oh, right," I said. "Jeanine got hold of you."

Larry went from bright- to brighter-eyed.

"God, she's awesome! She crushed me for an hour and a half, then we went out for big salads and protein smoothies. You left me there without a ride, you know."

I blinked. "I did, didn't I?"

"You're the best friend I ever had."

It was a wondrous bloody world. "So," I said, "all things jake for this p.m.?"

"Whatever," Larry said. "You can only worry so much, then you let it all go."

"Fatalist, eh? Good, I hate a Pollyanna." I wondered where Carrie's little bug was.

"Dude," Larry said, "we all gotta go out sometime, the four of us. Jeanine really likes you, and she'll love Carrie." He pulled closer and muttered, "I explained to her about Deborah."

Bloody wondrous, and not a little dangerous, I suspected. I checked Larry's bruises, now fading.

"Let's get through this afternoon, shall we, old man?" I started toward the door.

"Fay says... "

I whirled. "Yes?"

His look was hard to read. I waited on it.

"We're done, me and her," Larry said. "She says she wants to save me from myself."

"Ah," I said. "And how you feeling, then?"

He let out a big breath. "Bad, after she said it. But since yester... but now I'm fine."

I smiled at him. "You look rising fine indeed, pal. And will be." I turned again toward the door.

"She's... "

"Yes?"

"She's smarter... " Larry caught and corrected himself. "She's wiser than I am, Chest. And so are you."

It was positively time to go.

"No one's smarter than you, old fish. The wisdom comes from the knocks we get. Cheerio."

***

Sig Muck predicted Larry's gutting. Carrie was hotfoot to head that off. Should I believe a grobby degenerate ghost, or believe my own sneaky sense that the day might be saved after all? It was a crucial question.

There wasn't time in any event to call off Carrie's scheme now. There were, however, three minutes to float by Muck's office before my class finished lunch.

She was standing in her door, watching the lunch crowd pass. I first glanced past her to the desk, so near yet so far, then stepped up to the woman herself.

Fay Muck smiled at me, for the benefit of the young public passing by, then said for my ears only, "So what're you up to? No good as usual?"

Perhaps she was nerved-up and wary, but to me the words were a bit of the good old jousting.

"Just sighting the year's finish line now, Ms. Muck. Thinking what a super bunch we have here, from the top down. How good it all is, really."

161

Her smile hardened into a bit of a fright mask. "And you aim to keep it that way, is that it?"

I shrugged. "Out of my hands, init? All will surely come right, because everyone's so worthy."

Fay Muck was lean as a dancer. It seemed months since we'd talked. "Stay the hell out of it, and maybe it'll come right."

"Absolutely," I said. I dropped my own mask of nonchalance, and risked it. "You doing okay? Anything you need, just anything?"

Fay Muck stiffened, and dropped the smile. "Yeah," she said. "I need summer to get here, like yesterday."

I was mortified to feel myself reddening. "I -- "

"You're late to get your class," Fay Muck said. "Get 'em outta there so the ladies can clean up."

"Righto."

***

The year's lessons being in the barn, I slipped two aides a tenner each to take both my and Carrie's kids out for kickball. The aides would have a sunny good time, as well as a profitable, since Czarnecki would be captive in the tech lab, and not killing the joy of sport.

Carrie's room was on the same side as the lab, the windows facing out onto a big expanse of grass and playing fields. As I looked out, the two classes, pubescent June sixth-graders and wee kindergarteners, were assembling on adjacent pitches.

"All right," Carrie said, turning on the receiver from Radio Shack. I sat uneasily beside her on the corner of her desk. "They should be getting started."

"I hope you didn't pay Pentagon prices, love," I said.

"Hush!"

Some rustling and bumping crackled through the receiver. Then Fay Muck's rather distant voice:

"Awright, children, Mister Berkowitz, don't mind me. Just have a nice lesson and I'll sit here." A desk squealed.

Larry cleared his throat, once, twice. I sensed his new brio dissolving into panic. The Battle of La Boucherie had after all become a close-run thing, once Larry froze like a box of Green Giant peas.

"Mmm... errr... ahh... Okay! Everybody got their desktop showing?"

"Yay-ess!" chorused the girls.

"Is your d--ktop showing?" muttered Dylan Czarnecki.

Carrie and I exchanged looks.

"Ha-hem! Now, how do we get to Internet Explorer?"

"Excuse me!" Fay Muck said. *"Did I hear -- "*

"Click Start!" said a girl.

"Click F--t!" said Czarnecki.

"Hey!" Fay Muck said.

"Now, Dylan," Larry said mildly. *"Right, click Start and what do we have?"*

"Internet Explorer!" said the girls.

"This is kindergarten s--- ," said Czarnecki.

"We're just getting started," Larry said, *"and watch your language, please."*

"You heard him," Fay Muck said.

"I'll think about it," Czarnecki said.

I was watching Carrie. Her darling jaw worked tensely.

"Okay!" Larry said. *"Let's get online!"*

"Double-click!" said a girl.

"Duh," said Czarnecki.

"Just do it," said Fay Muck.

"Did you say 'Just do me'?" said Czarnecki.

Carrie Hahn had her hand on Walkie. But who the deuce had Talkie?

"Okay," Larry said, *"everybody got their Yahoo page up?"*

"Yay-ess!"

"Boo-hah."

"See Google?"

"Yay-ess!"

"Booger," Czarnecki said, using the long double o.

"You're cruisin', Czarnecki," Fay Muck said. *"I'm sorry, Mister Berkowitz, continue."*

"Ummm... err... Okay!" Larry said. *"You're going to do a little search now, based on two words I'm about to give you. The two words are--"*

"You s--k."

Carrie Hahn stood, walked ten paces across her room, and put Walkie to her mouth. Seeing this, I lost the thread for a moment, though Fay Muck ejaculated something, the girls said *"Dylan!"*, and Larry used the phrase "climate change."

"Now," Larry said, *"I want each of you to search and select a real good article you could use for a paper on climate change."*

"Ver-ry inneresting," said Fay Muck.

Carrie was muttering into Walkie. Several seconds passed of only ambient sound.

THE CHESTERFIELD HOURS

"Okay," Larry said, *"by now you should be looking at so much good stuff you might need to narrow your search, and maybe someone can find a good graph or other visual."*

"Check it out!" Czarnecki said. *"Jenna Jameson's pregnant!"*

Something strangled came out of Fay Muck.

"All right, Dylan," Larry said. *"I'm shutting you down."*

"Why? Cuz you're a f-g?"

"That's it!" Fay Muck yelled, and a chair screeched.

Carrie said into Walkie, "It's going down! Go, go, go!"

A paleish mass, with dark parts, moved against the green fields in the corner of my vision. I turned and looked out the window. Pandemonium blared from the receiver.

Across the lawn, sprinting toward the building, came the dogs Daisy and Cyrus, followed by the lad Nathaniel holding two leashes. Nathaniel called out something to the dogs, who just charged ahead.

Only seconds had elapsed, too little time even for Larry to seize Czarnecki's mouse, before the two dogs were just outside the tech lab window. There on the grass outside, they – big Cyrus and little Daisy – broke into the most blood-curdling, howling, and vicious combat since Old Yeller with the bear. Cyrus knocked Daisy galley-west, only to have her gather and fling herself at his throat.

"Sheesis Kay Reist!" Fay Muck screamed through the receiver. *"What the hell is that?"*

The two classes of children, big and little like the dogs, came running across the field. The dogs continued to lock up like gladiators and yelp, growl, and snap in horrifying violence.

I was on my feet. One thing I saw through the slaughterous tumult was this: the dogs took no toll on each other. For all the sound and fury, no flesh was torn. In fact, their tails were wagging as they "fought." Right. I left Carrie behind and got outside.

My own dog took no heed of me at first, but Nathaniel came bounding up. The children were gathering round, as the dogs continued to roar, squeal, slaver and struggle.

"Pretty artful, your black magic with critters," I shot quietly at Nathaniel, who stood now like a mannequin with the two leashes over one arm. "You're through practicing on mine, though."

Fay Muck, the two girls, and Larry streamed out onto the grass, Larry looking quite manful with Dylan Czarnecki by the collar.

"Daisy, come!" I commanded. The naughty corgi detached herself from Cyrus and trotted to my side.

"Come, Cyrus!" Nathaniel could only say now, and all went quiet...

"This is unacceptable!" Fay Muck bellowed at the top of her lungs.

Carrie Hahn, who'd been shutting down operations, appeared now in the door.

I did not belong there. Carrie, mastermind though she was, at least was next-door neighbor. I was from another wing, and in Fay Muck's mind, always presumed guilty, *prima facie*.

La Muck turned on me, glared, and then looked to Carrie. "Wait a minute, I know botha these dogs now, and something stinks here!"

Then she saw Nathaniel, who returned her look with a like amazed recognition.

Oh no, bloody no, I thought.

"Who's this wimp?" Dylan Czarnecki demanded of Fay Muck.

"That's all," Larry said, and with his new physicality dragged Dylan over to his sixth-grade peers.

"Ladies," he told the aides, "please take the children inside now."

Betty-Ann, the toughest of the aides, took Dylan from there, and next minute it was all supposed grown-ups, and dogs, standing round.

Carrie had slipped back inside -- out of discretion perhaps, yet it was a fatal blunder. It left the dog known to be hers in the hands of Nathaniel, who was clearly known by...

Splat!!

Nathaniel was on the ground, holding the side of his face. Larry stood over him, rubbing his right fist.

"That's Old Testament justice," Larry said. "A black eye for a black eye."

"Explain yourself!" I said.

Fay Muck had also slipped away. Daisy and Cyrus stood by, nuzzling each other.

"I don't know who he is," Larry said. "But he sucker-punched me a week ago when I... ah, forget it."

"Right, when you pulled him out of the Muck," I said. "Now say sorry. Get up, Nathaniel. It's all over now."

"Sorry, kid," Larry said. "I coulda stomped you, but I only owed you the one shot."

Nathaniel gingerly accepted Larry's hand. "That woman is bad news," he said.

"For some people," I said.

THE CHESTERFIELD HOURS

LET'S GET OUT OF HERE

Larry got tenure. Carrie got the sack. The American public education system, it hardly needs saying, is on shaky pins.

It was an eerily quietish final week. Naturally I tended closely to Carrie. What a doozy of a one-two combination she'd been biffed with!

Ironically, it was Nathaniel's obsession with Carrie that brought him into Muck's reach. The obsessed lover will follow, and peek, and listen, and sniff, and touch, and follow... and dog-walking allows one to follow more than the dog. It took him all the way to school. Fay Muck naturally would investigate. Leashed to a then-apparently generic yellow lab was a virginal likely lad... well, we all are fallen.

"Once we get to the Finger Lakes," Carrie said on Wednesday, "I may never leave. And not let you leave either."

Two days, and I couldn't wait. "'Tis a pity we're poor. I'd like to chuck it all, as a matter of fact. But I need my bloody job."

She just looked at me and smiled.

Stiff upper lip and all that, but I felt bursting with happiness. Look what I had, without money. See how Deborah was whipping herself toward that undiscovered country of wealth, the pangs of despised love... she could have it...

I came back to myself. Carrie still gazed at me placidly.

"You're *not* poor, are you, love?"

168

Her shy maidenness returned, and she looked down. "I am poor. My parents are not."

"Ah. Their own Finger, and all that?"

"Not quite."

It was no time for fantasy. "Well, I shan't hire on as their groom," I said, "assuming the stables are working ones."

She grasped my hand. "Just hire on as *my* groom, before I turn into Fay."

***

For Larry's sake, Carrie declined to rat out Fay Muck. She didn't, then, need her own bloody job.

Thursday brought a surprise.

"I'm going!" Larry Berkowitz said. To the Lakes, that is.

"That's ripping, old man," I said. And I meant it. "But haven't you gotten quite devoted to Jeanine – er, quite devoted to your workouts?"

Larry caught the slip.

"You're right," he admitted. "I probably wouldn't go if Jeanine was at the gym. But she went to a competition in AC and stuck me with some muscle-brain guy for the next few days."

I smiled. "And won't hearts grow fonder in her absence."

Larry blushed. "I hope hers does. Mine, don't even worry about it."

I clapped him on the shoulder. "Lake breezes, horsey rides, good food and local wine. You'll be fit as a champ when next she sees you."

***

Friday, getaway day, was full of parents and game-playing. Dylan Czarnecki was by then expelled. He'd be inflicted upon, er, promoted to junior high anyway, but would not receive a sixth-grade diploma. In being thus bereft, he joined me and everyone else born before cradle to grave prizes.

The final day, then, was casual but indistinct, gauzy, and interminable. Carrie, Larry and I were all packed, and Carrie's car loaded, for the long drive to a late dinner at her parents'.

As the clocked ticked down to 3:00, there came a school-wide sort of shifting about, as when soldiers drop weapons and wander into No Man's Land once armistice news sweeps through the trenches.

With my students taking up backpacks and going with parents, I took the long walk down the hallway toward Fay Muck's office. On my eerie way I noticed locker numbers, dust on the fire extinguisher, a crayon drawing of Carrie Hahn by a first grader who still adored her. I felt I'd never pass this way again.

The secretary Effie had straggled off into her own No Man's Land. I saw her just outside the side entrance, smoking. Fay Muck's voice, a bit nasal, composed but loudish, wafted from out of the auditorium down the hall and around the corner. The office was deserted.

"Hey, Chest!" Larry called. "The car's out front. Let's go!"

I said nothing as I slid past Effie's desk into Muck's office. As time froze and the most trivial particulars stuck out, I noticed a pair of women's winter boots sitting beside a wooden coat stand. January winds had blown fast and frosty when I first spoke to Carrie Hahn as more than a senior colleague...

I needed to be going. The desk just sat there like an inscrutable ark. I pulled at the drawer handle. A paper showed itself, with laboratory letterhead. There was general noise in the hallways but no *click-click* of spiked Muckian heels.

I took up the paper, and goggled with disbelieving eyes at the ghastly grobby facts thereupon. Back it all went into the drawer.

I was moving away, accelerating through the hall toward the main entrance. Larry still stood there.

"C'*mon* already!"

"Get in the car," I said.

Larry took the back seat. Carrie was at the wheel.

"What is it?" she said. "You're white as a sheet."

I got in beside her. "Get pointed northwest!" I said. "Away!"

Carrie threw it in gear. "We have to get the dogs!"

"By a merciful Provvy, and a good vet, the poor beasts'll never know what humans get up to."

"Huh?" Larry said.

I watched the good old school roll past and get behind me.

"Blood tests have caught out Dylan Czarnecki. Drive, I say!"

END BOOK TWO

Book Three

THE END OF THE BEGINNING

THE CHESTERFIELD HOURS

Part One

THE LAKE DISTRICT

All will be revealed, I told myself, if you only look and listen. Don't ask, or you'll only reveal yourself.

Carrie Hahn, at the wheel beside me, said, "There's always a city or town at the top and bottom of each lake. Like, we just passed Ithaca -- "

"Bottom of Seneca Lake!" Larry Berkowitz piped up from the back seat.

"No, Cayuga!"

"The frigging sign points north to Seneca Falls! So it's gotta be top of Seneca Lake!"

I turned round. "Are you quite all right, boyo? Want a cookie? Need to go wee?"

"He doesn't deserve a cookie," Carrie said.

Larry sat with the sleeping dogs Cyrus and Daisy piled on and against him.

"Are we there yet?" he squeaked, with a smirk on his face. "You two think I don't get it."

"Of course you get it, pally. You do deserve a cookie."

"Thanks."

"We haven't got any."

And so our motley quintet pushed happily northwest, four hours' ride behind us and closing on our destination. Only God and Carrie Hahn knew where that was. But we were in amongst the Lakes.

Carrie's parents awaited us.

Don't ask... don't wonder... all will be revealed...

***

When we got to the "top" of the lake, it was a different lake. In fact it was Seneca this time, as the highway, like a hypotenuse, cut the distance between the two largest and parallel Finger Lakes. The City of Geneva, top of Seneca, wasn't trading spots with Seneca Falls merely to unclog Larry's conundrum.

We chugged west a bit along "Old U.S. Route 20" – had Kerouac done that one? After half an hour we hit the City of Canandaigua, top of – no conundrum there – Canandaigua Lake.

Geneva and Canandaigua, as cities, are the novella form, the nicer for being just twenty-thousandish. One is relieved of the vexatious padding-out parts.

"Canandaigua means 'The Chosen Spot'," Carrie said, in patient kindergarten tones.

"In Yiddish?" I asked. Very bad of me, even to joke at this till the parents were well met.

Carrie shot me an adorable stink-eye. As she took a left around the lake, Canandaigua's downtown, running straight downhill to the water, disappeared over our right shoulders.

"If it's The Chosen Spot," Larry said, "how come your parents didn't choose it?"

"Shut up! We totally live in the Township of Canandaigua."

"The Indians chose downtown, old man. White millionaires choose West Lake Road."

"You shut up too! The Indians chose the whole thing. Native Americans, rather."

"The Indians call themselves the Indians, love. I like to be correct."

I turned again to Larry. "Only Tahoe's more expensive, for lakefront property. Number Two, nationally, is right here. Staggering wealth on this shore."

"Oh, are you gonna get it," Carrie said.

"Right," I continued to Larry, "the first Google search of my life, not a day ago, was for West Lake Road, Canandaigua."

I turned to see Carrie's knuckles growing whiteish on the wheel. "You couldn't have," she said.

"Google thy parents? Never, as I am a gentleman. Only the road."

"That's bad enough!"

Such by-play helped allay what really was becoming an all-overish case of nerves. We must be very close now. The lake on our left, now an unearthly azure blue, was said to change minute by minute from azure to silver to green, even to brown, and back. Scintillating...

Then there welled up out of the lake an effusion of white sails and lovely old boats. It was a marina, and besides the sailboats, both in and out of the water, there were Boston Whalers and burnished wood cabin cruisers – none of those low-rent bass-boat contraptions.

A mile down the lake Carrie turned right onto a private road, and next we were rising a steepish hill, the lake to our backs. There were no other houses now; instead along the hillside there ran row upon row of wired parallel vines, green and golden under the bluest sky Provvy ever painted.

"What're those?" Larry said.

"Grapevines," I said. "Grapes attach to them."

"My father's wine grapes, thank you," Carrie said. "Which is to say, we're here."

Into view came a great stone house, and behind it a red barn and smaller out-buildings with brown shingles perfectly faded as one sees them on Cape Cod. On each side of the road, very white fences began where the land leveled off. The grapevines split off around the fences and ran on forever. The fenced area to the left had a worn oval path perhaps an eighth-mile in circumference. The right fenced area held two horses, one a classic chestnut thoroughbred, the other an old pony.

"Empie and Maude," Carrie said with a caught-up emotion.

"Empie for Emperor, of course," I said.

"Of the Sun, right," she replied. "He's grown up since I went off to college. Maudie's ancient, I grew up with her."

The great house's black door opened and a tall silver-haired man emerged, followed by a lissome woman with long blonde hair streaked brown and silver.

Carrie parked on the grass halfway round a circle that faced the large porch, or "gallery." Hastily she jerked the parking brake, even as she was nearly out of the car. Next she flung the left rear door open, releasing Cyrus, who bounded off and over Larry as if he were an L.L. Bean doggy bed.

176

THE CHESTERFIELD HOURS

I held a hand on Daisy, who rested easy even with the door hung open. As I watched Carrie leap into the arms of the silver-haired man, I felt for a naked moment as if my heart had flown from my chest. Silly ass, I scolded, and re-composed myself.

I slipped a leash on Daisy, opened both front and rear passenger's side doors, and stepped out into a gorgeous hyper-reality. The cool air smelt fiercely fragrant of grass, pine, something else ineffable. The lake spread out below us, a blue bowl more metallic than the sky, bejeweled with white sails and bright boats.

The three Hahns' voices wove musically each round the other, the women's high and clear, the man's a low humourous baritone growl. I turned to face them.

The quite breathtaking mother devoured me with china blue eyes and a brilliant smile of God-given, regular teeth gapped in front. But only slightly gapped, to just that degree that makes a flusterating beauty. She was a lady too, if it need be mentioned.

The father like his wife wore elegant country clothes of denim, corduroy, hard-worked yet cared-for leather. Darkest of all of them, cool silver mane on a passionate Levantine head, he had a predatory wolfish aspect not unattractive in many men and some women. Brown/black eyes of a rueful, ironic cast did some to make him less frightful.

Speaking of, I sensed Larry hanging back in the car. But that was usual. Not a lad to ride with the Six Hundred, though the trainer Jeanine might yet bring him up to scratch...

"Sir," I addressed the father, who took my hand and nodded as he smiled. It was not, thank God, a hugging-strangers sort of family, but the mother was speaking now in a warm husky voice.

"Mr. Chesterfield," she said, taking my hand in both of hers. "We are *very* happy to have you up."

She was taller than Carrie, and tanner, with smile lines that any man of beating veins would gladly iron out with his nose. A thin gold watch gleamed tastefully on her light brown wrist.

"Your servant, madame," I said. Your slave, I thought, if not careful.

"Father," Carrie said, "*say* something. And Larry, get over here."

As I stood eye-to-eye with the older man, I heard Larry, with either head or shoe, clunk against the car.

"Shemp Hahn," the father said, in that low ironic growl, and offered a hand now to Larry who crept up and half-hid behind me.

"Who?" Larry burst out with an involuntary rudeness.

With a darted glance I pinned him like a butterfly, then slammed the book shut by turning back to Hahn the father.

"Friend Larry should know full well, sir, that it's an affectionate sobriquet, is it not, given to the child named Samuel, or Shmuel, who struggles in toddler years over enunciation."

The man turned up a half-smile and shrugged. "Could be. You seem to know a lot." He looked at his watch.

The mother with majestic intuitive sympathy said, "Why don't we all dress for dinner tonight? We've just got time, since you children will want to freshen up anyway, and Juanita's having everything ready at eight. What great fun!"

Alone perhaps amongst thirty-two year-old American males, I saw it just that way too. With Daisy sitting politely at my side, I gave a slight bow.

"You honor us, madame."

Dame Hahn suddenly had a brainstorm of recognition. "And welcome also, Mr. Larry! So pleased to meet you!"

Hearing Berkowitz thus addressed as a kiddie show sidekick, I judged the greeting sequence exhausted. I looked to Carrie. "We're to the stables, then, love?"

Carrie was regarding me with wide eyes, as if I was and wasn't in the scene with her.

"Oh yes," she said. "Come, boys, come, come."

We came, er, went.

REMIND ME NOT TO FIND YOU SO ATTRACTIVE

One does not, in America today, have the country-house experience every weekend. Firstly, who can provide it? Typically robber barons and Hollywood types have essayed it, from Newport to Santa Fe. But with all the glorious landscape that American Provvy provides, these types still don't build the genuine article. Nor do yoga and para-sailing seem as authentic as hunting the fox or murdering Lord Bletchley.

West Lake Road, however, was a revelation...

"If you came up to do some shooting," Shemp Hahn said from the head of the table, "you can go on down to the lake tomorrow, maybe shoot a fish, I guess."

Down the table Larry Berkowitz, who of course had brought no dinner clothes, gaped like a bass looking down the barrel. In sly anticipation, I had packed extra for my pal a never-worn gift from my late Granny Victoria. It was a herringbone tweed shooting jacket whose Size 42 shoulders over-topped the smaller man like a tent, and whose leather rifle pad 'twixt breast and shoulder was the exclamation point on a glaring *faux pas*.

I chuckled innocently at my host's gibe. "One thinks, sir, of Hemingway, his sharks, and his submachine gun. Getting for his bad sportsmanship, and God anyway loving the sharks more, a bullet through his own leg."

Larry, in snatching up his water glass, dinged it dissonantly against the wine glass. After taking a gulp, he looked accusingly at me.

"Well," said Barbara Hahn, the mother, "I think Larry is quite devastatingly debonair in it, and I won't hear a thing against him." With her left hand she patted Larry's right.

As a gentleman I would not put a pal in play like this if Larry had anything much at stake here. True, I needed a bit of cover for a really quite delicate passage, and this gave me some. The test would come, and need to be faced out, but punting it now into Day Two seemed quite right. Now I owed Larry some relief.

"Well, madame, we can chaff him a bit, because our Larry's quite the hot ticket just now. Saved a classroom from a vicious miscreant and got rewarded with tenure."

This felt jolly coming out, but as I looked across the table I saw Carrie's eyes welling moistly as of betrayal. Oh bloody hell!

She dropped her napkin, backed her chair out, and fled the room.

I was on my feet too. What a blunder to commit, after one mere glass of wine!

To follow her myself, married as I still was and in her father's house, was a bit pushing it. But follow I did, and up the stairs. I did not stop before I entered the room into which the girl ducked, filled with pictures of Carrie and horses, Carrie and classmates, Carrie and parents.

She had dived onto the bed, face down upon the pillow.

I did not dive after. There at least, decorum reasserted itself. I parked half a posterior onto the bed's edge and took Carrie's hand.

She turned her bleary face to me. "I haven't *told* them I didn't get tenure! Now you've messed things up."

I pressed her hand between both of mine and held the knuckles to my lips.

"I should have known it. People who talk all the time don't know anything. People like us, who don't talk, are supposed to just know. What a drunken swine I am."

She turned onto her back. Our eyes registered that we had never "been here" before.

"Are you drunk really?" She seemed to want me so. But did she want me to lie about it?

I only gave a gentle, ambiguous grunt. By remembering how not to talk, perhaps I'd start to "know" things again.

"Oh," she said, putting her hands round my neck, "let's just do what we want."

There was a creak from the stairs. With a hand under Carrie's lower back, I lifted her gently from the bed...

Well, we had kissed before. We had held hands, and snuggled on couches. But we had not kissed as we did now, standing, in the girl's oldest lair and sanctuary. It was better than talk, of course, and better even than knowing.

Barbara Hahn appeared in the doorway. My arms round Carrie, my chin in her hair, I stood facing the mother. It is to be inferred that from tip to toe I was presently "knowing" a thing or two.

"Why, children, what's wrong?"

Carrie's arms dropped from me but she did not turn. "Nothing, Mother."

All must do their duty now, above all the elders. The mother must needs return downstairs and withhold disapproval till alone with the daughter. The married, no doubt confused gentleman must withdraw, and the gentle maiden must modestly let arms and eyes drop floorward.

It is sad to report that only the youngest did her duty. Barbara Hahn in her emerald green dress walked brazenly forward. I, with nothing tending floorward, watched her approach as I stood clutching Carrie.

"You darlings," the mother said, covering my hand as it rested on Carrie's back. Then she kissed Carrie softly on the temple. "Come back to dinner. Nothing could ever be wrong." She was looking now at me.

Feeling Carrie's perfect little body in my hands, looking into the mother's china eyes and brilliant gapped smile, the blazing aureole of her lioness' mane, I experienced an Event...

"Oh, I say."

No decent narrative treats of such, but the better reader will gain sense by recalling the medical jargon phrase Cardiac Event, then imagining something further south that is the opposite of painful.

"Better said than done," said young Carrie in a frozen whisper.

"Really, do come," Barbara Hahn said. "Father and Larry will be missing us."

I still held to Carrie as if stuck, which embarrassed pose would by and by produce its own foreshadowed reality.

Carrie spoke more sharply. "We'll be right there, Mother. Please."

Barbara Hahn, still smiling at me, took a step back.

"Of course, dear. If Mr. Chesterfield can tear himself away." And then she was gone.

We lovers gingerly broke.

"Sorry, love. Have you... taken friendly fire?"

Carrie's eyes were drilling into mine. I'm for it now, I thought with chagrin.

"I dearly love you," she said instead.

"Forever!" I said, and reached for her again, to be met with a lovely stiff-arm to the chest.

"Down the back staircase!" she said, and took me by the hand. "We'll get you out back and changed in a jiffy!"

Well, we'd dashed pell-mell through kitchens before, it was our first romantic notion, and the housekeeper and cook Juanita whirled and clucked "Ah mi!" as we flew by and Carrie shoved me out the back door to the stables.

Minutes later I re-entered the dining room. My fresh sail-cloth chinos were the violent negative to the dark dress slacks I'd last been seen in.

Larry goggled at me in the old bassy way. Carrie and Barbara dipped demurely into their soup, the mother with a slight smile curling at her lovely mouth's corners.

Shemp Hahn only glanced up from his stuffed lamb chop.

"You guys are like broads already with the wardrobe changes."

VICE RISK

It was rising ten o'clock when we three men retired to the library. We sat in deep club chairs around a coffee table. Juanita brought brandy on a tray. Shemp Hahn handed Larry and me cigars the size of the old German hand grenades, gestured for us to use the long wooden matches on the table, and lit his own.

Freighted thus with snifter and tobacco, I found myself, in market lingo, overweight vice risk. My chosen hedge was to make short work of the brandy whilst going long cigar ash. I lit the massive heater, took a polite puff and placed it in a tray to grow white.

"So," Shemp Hahn said as he jetted smoke toward the ceiling. "What do you want from me?"

It was the unthinkable question to ask of a gentleman. Therefore I perfectly expected it, but I did not leap to answer. I toyed with the cigar, grinding it lightly in the tray. I was feeling very well. I wanted to be here, in this countryside, this township, this house, this room, this chair...

"Your daughter, sir, after a decent interval."

Shemp Hahn moved the great cigar around in his mouth, then pulled it out and jerked a look at Larry Berkowitz. "What's *your* story?"

Larry, bug-eyed, clutched both brandy and unlit cigar to his stomach with little alligator arms. "No story," he said.

"Good." Shemp Hahn turned back to me. "What's your wife got to say about this?"

185

My punt had been blocked, but at least back into my own hands. I could crumple piteously to the turf, or I could carry on. Is that not our life on earth?

"My wife, sir – a very fine woman – wishes to seek her fortune. I would have her do so."

Shemp Hahn, holding his cigar with forefinger wrapped over it, made a great wolf's grin.

"From what I hear, she don't have to seek. You're tossing it to her."

"He thinks you're a schmuck," Larry Berkowitz broke in.

From this one-two punch I again might have crumpled. And coming behind it was a finishing uppercut, the idea that my beloved Carrie would "talk" about the rumoured Fortune of my mother's family, the Ffoulkes...

"You said schmuck, not me," Shemp Hahn told Larry. "Thirty years ago I stopped talking like a street yid. I never quite got the British thing down, except for the property, but anyway I dropped some baggage along the way."

And what you gained thereby in dropping, I thought, was no bag at all. Barbara Hahn came warmly to mind...

Larry, looking portentously at me, said "So he doesn't say schmuck. He's still thinking it."

I didn't need brandy for my defense, but I anyway had swallowed it. I took up my cigar and puffed nonchalantly.

"The Fortune's illusory, sir, while your daughter, by the grace of God, is what she is."

Shemp Hahn, still composed, ironic, smiling, looked at Larry with something like tribal familiarity.

"How is he a schmuck if he wants Carrie and all this too?" He gestured with upturned hands to give a sense of "all this."

I by now was pretty warm, but I meant to match Shemp Hahn's cool.

"What I want is Carrie and none of 'this', sir. I pledged myself to your daughter months ago. Of 'this' I knew nothing till today."

Now Shemp Hahn looked amusedly over his other shoulder, and spit a bit of tobacco. "What are you, the Duke of Wales?"

I winced. "Of Windsor, sir, and hardly. With one hand he threw a crown away, and with the other sponged up a king's ransom. I am not he, sir."

Shemp Hahn, his cigar half smoked, squashed it out and dropped it into the tray. Then he stood.

"Yeah, okay, to be continued. How was the brandy?"

I also rose. "A good familiar friend, sir, and well used. Thank you."

Larry, rising and a bit baffled, added, "Yeah, thanks a lot."

Shemp Hahn was halfway to the door already. "Make sure you got everything you need out in the stables. We lock up real good at night." He turned, gave me a savage smile, and was gone.

TWO COTS AND A HOTTIE

Larry and I had two cots separated by a small table with a single lamp on it. I am a nightly bedtime reader, but I pushed the lamp over to Larry's side. Tonight I preferred my own story, and wanted to let the day's memory wash over me.

Daisy lay at my feet in the good old way. Tomorrow she would meet the horses, at least the more temperate Maude. I myself would not ride. Daisy and I would stay aground together, enjoying the good earth, the air, the jolly barnyard menagerie.

As Larry and I were turning in, Carrie called to us from the stable stairs.

"Come," I said.

She entered in a light flannel nightgown and slippers. The night was mild, cool, delightful, and so was she in this prim attire. She sat on Larry's cot, just friendlily. We had after all, the three of us, had a day of it together. But Carrie reached a hand toward mine.

"Mother and I talked, and there are no secrets left," she said. "Not about my job, not about The Fortune, not about us, or Deborah."

"The Fortune'll always be a secret," I said. "Make that a myth."

"Have it your way," she said. "But everything else came out, and do I feel lighter!"

I rolled onto my back and touched her flannelled thigh. "Things long suppressed can come out in a hurry. I'm rather lighter myself these past couple hours."

When she could no longer blush, she would no longer be Carrie Hahn. She turned and put a hand on Larry's shoulder.

"And," she said, "we'll have no secrets from Larry, nor he from us, eh?"

"She wants to meet Jeanine, old man."

Larry snorfed and turned onto his side away from them. "We're not dating, for cryin' out loud. I'm her... her client."

"And a very proper professional dominatrix/slave relationship it is," I said. "You'll never be better pounded, so don't go looking."

"Geez, lay off," came the muttered reply, and so we did.

I had a secret still, one that I'd tried to put right with Provvy, a-way back when Benedict Hoepplewhite was blighting our lives. But if poor wronged Jeanine could find happiness with Larry, that secret at last would die away atoned...

Suddenly the whole fantastical day seemed to come in on me with a silent crash...

"'Night, love," I murmured. "We'll have more of this tomorrow."

Woozily I felt her delicious lips on mine. "And there is more," I thought I heard her say. *"Much too much... too much... to tell you... tonight..."*

THE CHESTERFIELD HOURS

DAPHNE IN THE COUNTRY

Tink... a-dinka-link... a-linka-dink... a dinka-doo...

It was not, perhaps, quite so musical as that. But it was a tune that had got into my dreams before...

"Mother!" I shot up in my cot.

"Why so surprised, dear boy?" came the old familiar voice from near the screened window. "Are not my visits getting old hat by now?" The bourbon and ice clinked softly now.

Larry, deep in slumber, sawed away in the next cot. Daisy, in her calm acute way, was looking toward that window.

"Well," I said, groping for composure, heart pounding. "I can't... I can't believe you're so far from home, Mother. It can only mean... "

"That I've really actually snuffed it?" The bluish figure by the window shifted, the ice clinked, her ring glinted, and she sipped. "Let's have no more of that, eh?"

"Are you... quite all right?"

She tittered. "Having a ripping time! Do you recall Hardy's wonderful prostitute poem?"

"Vividly, Mother. I was no more than five when you read it me for a bedtime story."

"'One's pretty lively when ruined,'" Daphne recited. "Only think, dear. By being alive, I never got to see you throw a dummy in that French restaurant. What a priceless loss! Now I see the damnedest things."

One shouldn't redden with embarrassment whilst sitting in the dark talking with a ghost. But I did feel a warming in the cheeks.

"You weren't, Mother, haunting about the house earlier this evening?"

Daphne, sipping again, nearly spit her Manhattan. "Oh la! You dear children! You really must get on with the ceremony, and get in a garret together."

"I'm moving on it, Mother. Deborah's in effect bought from me a call option on The Fortune. All she has to do is chuck up our marriage, which for her is no premium at all to pay."

"Chuck up your marriage and then marry... that man. She should *collect* a premium from him, since by enjoying her favors he thinks *he's* the one gone to heaven."

I did not like to think about my father with Deborah. I would, however, lump it in order to have my Carrie.

"What could make her a better premium, Mother, than the whole bloody Ffoulkes Fortune, inherited by Dad from you? Wait! Are you trying to say... is The Fortune really bollocks after all... "

But Daphne's moonlit, bluish shape had begun to dissolve. Daisy, who had watched the shape so intently, put her head down and went to sleep. I myself felt a weird pull between drowsiness and panic. I dropped back onto the pillow...

"Why don't you answer, Mother?" I mumbled.

My eyes closed. The voice seemed saying, *"There are many events in the womb of time which will be delivered. Get you back to the metrop and take nothing for granted."*

Next came nothing but lake breeze through the screens.

THE CHESTERFIELD HOURS

SOMEONE'S IN THE KITCHEN, I KNOW

I didn't want to get back to the metrop – not now, in fact not ever. I'd weeks ago decided to let the Fortune go to the devil, er, Deborah. But more than that, somewhere between the brandy and bedtime, I'd decided I must visit Canandaigua town. It pulled at me. I would buy or rent and make my living there. I needed nothing from Shemp to dwell with Carrie in the Chosen Spot that made her...

But doesn't one defy a ghost at one's own risk? And, if that ghost gave you life, it is ungrateful and ungentlemanly into the bargain...

So my mind was conflicted when I awoke, with Daisy nudging me. Yet physically I felt topping, having slept nine hours. Larry was dressed and gone. I walked to the window and looked out upon the lake. It was another day of bluebird skies and bright but gentle sun, just pluperfectly Juneish.

Dressed, I descended with Daisy to the stables proper and noted the horses were out. I remembered, or thought I did, that Carrie had promised me "much more" today. But what was that against my ghostess's adamant marching orders?

Carrie was inside the white fence, atop the plodding Maude, with Cyrus walking beside them. Shemp Hahn and Larry Berkowitz stood outside together, leaning against the fence. At the sight of this scene, Daisy left my side and scooted right under the fence. Maude dipped her head just slightly to glance, and kept on walking.

Carrie spotted me and called "Wake up, you sleepyhead!"

I smiled and walked up to Larry's side. "Have done," I called back. "As you see."

"Go get some breakfast," she called over her shoulder as she circled away from me.

Bloody famished, I was. This country made you want take on fuel and burn it off as a furnace would. Likewise did it seem to work on one's erotic energies...

I tapped Larry's shoulder. "You've eaten, mate?"

"Tons," was the reply. "Go get some."

I turned for the house. To get fed here, you went to Juanita. But as all appetites seemed to converge here, it was Barbara Hahn in the kitchen door as I went to go get some.

"Good morning, Mr. Chesterfield!" She wore her jeans and boots, with a light plaid flannel shirt, her hair back in a ponytail. "You must be starving."

"Quite. But I'm terribly sorry if Juanita has been kept waiting on me. I wouldn't want that, madame."

Across the counter island the cook moved briskly about, taking on, taking off, putting away.

"Don't be silly," Barbara Hahn said. "We're both anxious to get you properly fed, aren't we, 'Nita?"

"Ah, si, si."

Feeling Barbara's graceful tanned hand at my back, guiding me to a chair, I experienced an eerie sensation. I was still feeling Daphne Ffoulkes Chesterfield's bluenight command. Now as I sat with this vivacious younger/older lady, myself possessed of the same body as the young Jack

193

Chesterfield, I had the weird sense of being at my parents' improbable first meeting...

"Dear man, you're all at sea. What is it?"

It is deeply disconcerting to be transparently read like this. What if an enemy were to so read one?

I focused my eyes with determined neutrality on Barbara Hahn's blue ones. Then I surrendered to their oceanic sympathy.

"Madame, you are... so good, and... you have caught me out. There is something."

"Yes?"

Would Captain Jack have blubbered and blathered? Would Daphne have stood for it? But Barbara Hahn had both my hands in hers.

"Only a gelded hobbledehoy," I gritted out, standing again, breaking her gaze, wrestling with myself, "imposes his worries on a new acquaintance, and a great lady at that."

"Oh nonsense!" she said, pulling me face to face with her. "Out with it, before you burst! We are all friends now, and my daughter's in this to the limit!"

I eased back from her, as it was a fraughtish moment.

"Something's called me back to the city – touching on my late mother."

"Then you must go!" she said, releasing my hands and pushing out at my chest. "Father and I were so shocked to hear of your loss. Go, do your duty, dear boy!"

No words from an admired lady, not even "Come hither," are more compelling to the gentleman than "Go do your duty." Perhaps "Come hither and do your duty."

"I won't ruin everyone's holiday," I said. "But I can't just hop a bus or train. I've got Daisy."

Barbara Hahn turned and told the housekeeper, "Juanita, make us sandwiches, please."

She turned back to me and said, "I'm taking you home. Get your bag, get Daisy, and tell Carrie, but don't let her keep you."

***

The first two tasks were easily done. Daisy and I soon stood together in the driveway, both wolfing down food like, well, a pair of wolves. I had my bag beside me. Shemp and Larry were off in the vineyards. Barbara Hahn was in the garage. Carrie, of course, had been occupied with Maude. When she finally walked out of the stables, though, I recognized the good old war-path stride.

"What is my mother doing with you?" she demanded. Her perfect little jaw was set like a Buckingham Palace Guard's.

"Only helping in an emergency, love. You see, it's really about *my* mother."

"Your mother? She didn't mention an emergency to me."

This caught me off-guard. "She... visited you too, love?"

"Yes, but no emergency!" Carrie said. "She was totally boring, like 'What a charming place, how happy you children will be, such lovely parents,' yada yada yada. So she's holding back on me and you're running out!"

I took her in my arms. Barbara Hahn roared up beside us in a huge blue Range Rover, the biggest. To drive to the far metropolis and back again, in this, must require a pipeline to the House of Saud.

"I have such huge news!" Carrie cried. "And you're ruining it!"

I kissed her hard on the mouth. "I want to get going before Larry sees me. When will you return to the city?"

Carrie pulled away and turned her back on me. "How about never?" she said, voice muffled, her chin on her chest.

"Then I'll be back here," I said.

She turned back round. She did not smile but her green eyes glinted at me. "That's more like it."

"Can't you see he adores you?" Barbara Hahn called from the truck. "Now let him go, Carrie."

"You're a big help, Mother!"

This time I lifted her fully from the ground and placed kisses all round her cheeks, eyes, forehead and mouth. Then I dropped her feet first back to ground and spanked her away from me.

"I'll call for your huge news tonight, if able," I said. "Otherwise in the morning."

I popped Daisy into the Range Rover, then climbed in myself. "Teach Larry to ride, will you?" I called after Carrie. "It'll impress his new girl."

I slammed the door shut and we roared away.

THE CHESTERFIELD HOURS

HEART-STOPPING NEWS

I got my first look at Main St. Canandaigua only because it was on the way to the New York State Thruway. A mile uphill from the lake Barbara Hahn and I drove past a great cluster of old buildings, Colonial, Victorian, Federal, some residences, some churches.

"There," Barbara said, pointing to a gorgeous pile of grey granite and stained glass, "is where you and Carrie will be married."

St. John's Episcopal Church, the sign read.

The gallant reader who has made the long slog with this narrative will understand this moment for what it was.

"Long live you, madame, and your husband," I said. "Bless you both, yes we will."

And, having said nothing of it heretofore, I said nothing more.

***

And the two of us, it seemed, privately determined we would not talk overmuch on this long journey. There would be time, there would be time...

And there was time enough, in such a long journey, for me to wonder if I had jerked the weekend apart for everyone – all over a dream. A dull panic came on as New York State fled past us. Did I need now to hunt up a crisis to justify myself to this fine lady, for her time, her gas, her infinite kindness? Throw a crisis at her feet, to buy her belief in my seriousness?

The hours and miles passed. I insisted on filling the Land Rover with gas. Once inside the metropolis, we drove past Carrie's flat, superstitiously almost. Then to my Cape Cod. I offered it to Barbara Hahn for freshening, for coffee, for anything. She went upstairs. By the time I'd put out food for Daisy, Barbara was descending the stairs.

"Well," she said. "I must leave you to your family business."

Ragged, guilty almost, I said "Do rest a bit. I'm... I'm not sure what I'm to do, honestly."

She looked at me perplexed. After all, a ghost, nothing else, had told me get home.

She said, "You have messages, I see."

The phone in fact was flashing. It can be a grave mistake to play phone messages in front of anybody, intimate or stranger. I was perhaps too ready to let Barbara Hahn in...

I didn't care. I jabbed the Play Message button. Barbara Hahn, in clear hearing range, made a discreet turn of her back to the phone.

"You selfish, irresponsible bastard," Deborah's voice said. *"You refuse to get a cell phone, you go off with your little sparrow where you can't be reached, and your father has a heart attack. The divorce papers are ready anyway, and I'm bringing them to the hospital, because I so cannot wait."*

She gave the room number and hung up.

END BOOK THREE, PART ONE

Part Two

JACK O' HEARTS

Deborah's "I so cannot wait" – for divorce – was so 21st century, so adolescent, and so tortured with entwined motive. For her, a golden clock was somewhere ticking, like an old man's heart beneath guilty floorboards.

We all of us have clocks a-going, I thought, one example being my and Carrie's hammering wish to at last "get at it." But for Deborah, Fortune, not flesh, was the mainspring. Sluttish time, importunate desire. I hung up the tattletale phone and turned to my noble future mother-in-law, who'd just heard her daughter aspersed.

"My house is yours," I told her. "To rest in, for a meal, to sleep over. Or if you need to get back… "

She came to me and took my hands. "Nonsense, dear boy, I'm driving you to the hospital. You're distracted."

I of course had my own car now, in the garage. I needn't drag Barbara Hahn into this.

But she was the all-in type, and I wanted her in.

"Right," I said. "Let's go."

***

As we entered the hospital, Barbara dropped back behind me. Perfectly smart, that. I let her drift, allowing her to observe without getting spied with me.

It occurred to me that Barbara might want a piece of Deborah – also that my guv'nor might have landed here through just the same motive, more amorously derived.

We reached Jack Chesterfield's room with Deborah nowhere apparent, and Barbara strolled on by and continued down the hall.

My father did not notice me at first. I noted the old man's ruddy but perfectly normal complexion, his easy breathing and still powerful chest as he lay with head propped up by two pillows. Before I could speak I felt Barbara Hahn at my side, slightly behind me, and turned to see her looking with radiant calm at Jack, who now turned to us. I opened my mouth to speak, and at that moment felt Barbara leave us.

"My God!" Captain Jack said. "Who was that?"

I eased my way in.

"For one thing," I said, "another man's wife. For another, the first manifestation in you of buyer's remorse, which touching on Deborah is no idle metaphor. How are you?"

"My ticker's gone on the bum!" Jack's eyes were clear but anguished.

I slightly snorted. "It hasn't. You've got the heart of a young Labrador retriever, and lately the brains. If you can pull yourself together you'll chuck away those revolting crack-arse PJs and directly walk out of here."

"Well, *something* happened!" the old man said. He was, I say again, the picture of health but frantic in spirit.

"Something happened, but not that," I said. "To paraphrase Mother, a gentleman never infarcts in bed."

The Captain nearly convulsed. "How did you know… your mother! In bed! Wha… your mother!"

"Of course it happened in bed," I said, "Deborah rogering you right into this place. I hadn't a doubt. What about Mother?"

"I *saw* her, son!" Jack stopped straining and seemed to sink back into his pillows. "I saw her," he repeated weakly, and closed his eyes.

"Saw her where?"

Jack lay still, as if embalmed. "Over… like you said… over Deborah's shoulder. Then I woke up here."

"There's a pretty picture," I said. "Where's the Marine in you, first taking the bloody bottom, then fainting away like an anorexic ballerina."

Jack opened his eyes, indignant. "Well, if your Mother hadn't -- "

"I hope it amused her, anyway," I said. "Where is Deborah?"

"She went out for coffee."

"Coffee with whom? Never mind."

Barbara Hahn slipped back into the room, so silently that I saw it first in Jack's widening eyes.

"Ah," I said, "this is Carrie's mother, Mrs. Hahn. Madame, my father."

A patient typically has people bellowing at him like carnies. Yet everything men bleed for came out in Barbara Hahn's four hushed words. "However are you feeling?"

Better and better, I judged, as the brawny Captain, saying nothing, climbed from the bed, stood at attention—rather fully at attention – and saluted.

"Right," I said, and turned to Barbara Hahn. "He's a terrible show-off, madame. But he does show up, I'll say that."

Barbara and I then cheesed it, as there'd be a better time and place for Deborah and her papers.

QUICKIE DIVORCE

Those papers needed no peddling to me, as I was braced to get on with it. Jack would be at least another night in hospital, and if that spurred Deborah to greater urgency, I felt very fine about it.

Barbara Hahn decided that she would leave town directly. She did not actually want a piece of Deborah. There is a lesson for our young people in this. Petty as Deborah's phone jape at Carrie had been, Madame Hahn knew that she had stumbled into other people's business. It was, as the phrase has it, "not about her." Legions today should take that lesson.

That is hardly to suggest that Barbara had fear. Just let Deborah bring that rot round West Lake Road...

It was late afternoon. We were back at the good old Cape Cod. Barbara stood in the front hall holding her Range Rover keys. I thought she must have a very great stamina to do this. It seemed in fact to be pushing it...

"I say, madame, stay in town tonight." I took from my own ring a key to Carrie's flat. "I appreciate your wanting to stand clear. But within 24 hours I shall likely be divorced and my father released. And Carrie shall return."

I paused and handed her the key. "It seems a shame, and a hardship."

Barbara Hahn pocketed the key and embraced me. I floundered for a response. Hers was a body to enfold amorously, but that of course was not our relation. Yet I couldn't act the cold fish if I'd wanted to. I settled on a hugging sort of clinch with my right hand spread across her back ribs, my left in a curving sort of place near the hip. And she kissed me near, but not on the mouth, then stepped back.

"What fun!" she said. "You thrash out your business and I'll lay low back at the hideout!"

No wondering where Carrie got it, the love of capers. The father was no square either…

"Right," I said. "If Carrie calls I'll put her onto you. Now get you out of sight and behave till I call."

As I said this I barely stopped myself spanking her away as I had Carrie, and I wondered what'd come over me, to treat a great lady as though we were in *Georgy Girl* together.

But Barbara Hahn left quite in the spirit of the thing.

***

Deborah called twenty minutes later. I was pen-ready, and the terms as I understood them were generous. That is to say, I would live in the house till it was sold, whereupon I'd get half the proceeds. There would be no alimony, and we'd keep our respective retirement accounts. I had held to my gentleman's code and acceded to my wife's wishes. The divorce was uncontested, amicable, cheap, routine…

… all because I was tacitly allowing her to fly to Jack and share in everything yet to come to the widowed Captain. Thus after the "heart attack," Deborah was evermore impatient.

No narrative of even middling literary worth has lawyers in it. Not anyway since Trollope and Dickens, and Dickens at least would slay off the wicked blighters once they'd done their bit to goose the plot. My man had vetted the arrangement – that will suffice for our purposes.

Deborah came to the house in t-shirt and sweatpants. Her auburn hair was unwashed and pulled back, not in the sporty cowgirl way of Barbara Hahn's ponytail. It struck me that I hadn't seen my wife in such dishevelment in many a moon. It didn't matter...

"Welcome, dear. Dad still resting comfortably?"

Standing there in the front hall Barbara Hahn had just left, Deborah seemed trying to read me. Daisy came and sniffed round her, but Deborah, having given the dog over too, did not bend.

"Last I checked," she replied.

"Before coffee, was that?" It just popped out, I couldn't have it back, and naturally she got shirty about it.

"You think I've been sitting on my a— ? I'm the one doing everyone's legwork."

"I know, dear, of course." I gestured to the living room, the sofa and coffee table. "Shall we?"

Perhaps on the battleship *Missouri* signings have drama. Most do not. We signed. What was there to say?

We stood. "Love you as always, dear," I said. "We are all still family, what?"

At this she gave out a bit. "I've got to get back to him," she said. We hugged without kissing.

"Right," I said. "Go and do your duty."

With a gasp she let something escape her, but with a sniff she got it partly back, and it went without words, unrecoverable.

GAUDY AWFUL NIGHT

Carrie of the huge news called that evening.

"Your mother's staying over tonight," I told her directly.

"What?"

"In the metropolis, that is. At your flat, I mean to say."

"Put her on the phone."

"What? Look here, love, by at your flat I mean at your flat. She's at your flat. Call your own phone."

"I will. Why did you go home today?"

"What's your huge news?"

"I asked first."

"Well, Mother popped in a-haunting on Dad and Deborah. Put him in hospital with a fainting spell they took for a heart attack. That's of course why she told me get home, and -- "

"Okay, I get the picture. I'm going to call my mother now."

"And your huge news is?"

"Tell you tomorrow, in person."

"Oh I say, love, dirty pool now -- "

Click.

"I'm divorced," I said to the dead phone. "That's *my* bloody huge news."

***

Later I lay on the good old rack, Daisy at my feet. There were no lake breezes, but even in the metrop it was June all the same.

There weren't words for the two days past. Only yesterday I'd taught my last class in Fay Muck's Gomorrah – but nobody else knew yet.

And now a new life. Was the future really now so free and clear? Today's poor reader may take up this narrative for diversion from a new and gathering darkish age. She might, even yet, feel the halcyon mid-'00s trustily at her shoulder like a boon companion, when it's all falling back now...

But we are ever living with our worries, and always surprised by joy. In the days of this narrative I could expect a quick sale and ample cash even for half the house proceeds. Yet then as now, chucking up a real job might mean settling for a paper-hattish one. You had better know there will be joy...

I lay staring at the ceiling. Now that I had determinedly put The Fortune from me, I felt certain of its existence. Anecdotal strands tugged at me. When I thought of the absurd shooting jacket from Granny Vic, I could not gainsay its elegant workmanship, couldn't deny it was quite the real thing. And the stalwart long-slogging reader will recall that Daphne on The Night of the Third Manhattan had told *something* to animate Deborah.

I had no visitor this night. Ghosts do not come when you wait up for them.

"Well, Mother," I said to the ceiling, "your antics of yestreen have quite pushed the pawns around. And I am one of them."

I had unspent energy. Should Barbara Hahn need me to come put out a fire, I would answer the call. But she did not call...

No Ffoulkes had ever betrayed a hint of wealth. Then again, The Fortune if it existed never came to one whose race wasn't largely run. You don't put on the dog when you no longer can walk the dog.

Deborah, though, was a different animal altogether. She'd put it on, swank it about...

I was falling into a doze. If a ghost wants to appear, she appears, instanter. She is not detained at the baggage carousel...

...yet in my dream I saw Daphne traipsing through the night from the Lakes, a trap in each hand, hailing Mr. Pickwick's heavenly post-chaise.

SUNDAY

When you go to sleep so wound-up, you do not reap the pure, restorative dreamless. You will instead awake just staggering into Athens from Marathon, and if you have drunk the wrong whisky you will have been running *from* things slavering and bestial.

I had not drunk that whisky, so I awoke feeling just jet-laggish. Yet my mind had come round on a couple things. Sleep is a mysterious process.

I had not mourned my mother. She hadn't let me.

Yet I missed her. She could not hug and kiss me, couldn't fry me bangers and fuss with my guv'nor in the good old way at brunch. And in losing Daphne, I had largely lost my father.

Barbara Hahn would be my mother now. That was agreeable – more than. There was something else, but the impatient reader will be wanting movement, as did I myself...

By 9 a.m. I'd already walked Daisy and heard from Carrie, whose small, not huge news was that she and Larry were already on the Thruway.

Right. I, sick of lachrymose reflection, was now for action. I left Daisy in house and drove to the hospital.

"Chesterfield's the name," I told the desk nurse, "here to take home my father John."

"Okay," she said, checking her end. "He's ready. But there was a lady."

I smiled. "Right, a lady. Not wife, not daughter. I'm his only family, actually." I knew the room and was easing toward it. "Thanks awfully," I told the nurse.

The old guv'nor was dressed and pacing, looking like splitting a cord of firewood. "Well!" he said when the son entered.

"Well yourself," I answered. "Let's break out of this Bastille, what? Fancy a bite out in the open air?"

"But Deborah... "

"Deborah sleeps in on Sundays. Then the gym. You come third, old buffer, haven't you heard?"

Jack blinked in indignation. "I want to blow this dump!"

"What d'you think I'm here for? Carrie will be back by noon, and we're going to brunch *al fresco* with her and her mother. All right with you?"

The Captain's eyes went bright within his ruddy face. "Well, that'll be fine!"

"Of course it will be," I said. "Let's go."

***

We met up in that gritty part of the metropolis, lately gentrifying, that held old Italian bakeries, refrigerated warehouses, gymnasiums, and bright new cafes. One of the cafes had tables now outside, and that's where our jolly gang, of old and new acquaintance, convened.

Larry Berkowitz sat waiting for us in an outdoor chair.

"They got Wi-Fi inside this joint!" he called out, jerking a thumb backward toward the building.

Carrie and her mother had arrived together in the Range Rover. As my father and I crossed over the street, the Hahn women flowed to us like warming tropical waves.

I looked to Carrie's eyes for lingering peevishness. I quivered with love, wanted to sweep her from the ground. Of course a gentleman in public must wear the mask, but if his beloved should wish to tear it off...

Then she was in my arms – all forgiven.

"I've signed Deborah's potty papers," I whispered in her ear. "And love you very, very dearly."

Barbara Hahn of course did not leap at the Captain. But she took both his hands in hers in that way she had.

"How fit you look! You belong out of that silly cot!"

I gently cleared my throat. Captain Jack Chesterfield these fifty years past had used silly cots in every kind of way, except to play the patient.

A gust of wind blew debris off the street.

"Are we losing the sun?" Barbara said. She wore a sleeveless summer dress under a light sweater of Scottish wool. With her astonishing sympathy she took the Captain by one arm. "Let's get you inside in the comfier chairs."

"Hey," Larry said. "Jeanine's gonna to join us on her lunch break."

"Super!" I said. "Nat Cole was wrong, you know, never to take his girl where the gang goes." Happiness is this, I thought. I had my father back, for an hour, for a day. I felt Carrie again in my bloodstream. Once more it was a world of pals and family, going forward...

It certainly smelt better inside. Would-be Prousts sat at laptops round the periphery, inspired to immortality by the aroma of trans-fat-free, high-fiber blueberry mini-muffins. It is to be hoped that excess hyphens did not transfer to the prose.

We took a table. You had to order from a queue at one of two registers. I said I would get us coffees all round, plus pastries.

"Get sandwiches too!" Carrie said, as I rose to go order.

I wanted to treat, but adding five sandwiches at this place would get steepish...

I must have grimaced, because Carrie added, "Mother will pay for the sandwiches."

"Let me first get us caffeinated, love. Everyone check the sandwich board and make an order list." Would the day ever come when I needn't worry the cost of things? No, it wouldn't, not now...

I chose the register with the shorter queue and soon found why. A shaggy-headed, heavyset bloke, a grad student type, was pleading about his credit card. These university sorts won't even pay cash for a Coke.

"I'm totally way under my limit," the young man whined. "This cannot be happening!"

The teenage clerk called in a manager. I sighed. The longer queue next me had only lengthened. I walked back to the gang and sat down. "Just the luck," I said.

"It's fine," Carrie said. "Try again when the line's shorter."

"Yeah," Jack said, chipper as a lad with Barbara Hahn at his side. "Take a load off, son."

On the other hand, I sensed a coolness between Carrie and her mother.

Across the room another young man, a bearded beatnik sort in a grey fedora, took up his own laptop and left by the side door. I paid him little mind. This was already more of grad types than I got in a fortnight.

Larry, however, took note of the departure and turned to me. "What's up with the kid at the register?" he asked.

"Oh," I said, "he's wielding a credit card with no credit. I say, try using currency just once for laughs." My ebullient mood was ebbing away.

Larry stood, and now stared at a table with a laptop on it, a hooded sweatshirt hung on the chair. The shaggy bloke's, perhaps.

"Excuse me," Larry said. He went to the short queue register, perhaps to puzzle it out for them, a Cyber Samaritan.

I left him to it. Bugger all technology, I was back with my Carrie, with my father, my new moth...

Barbara Hahn held a crisp hundred-dollar bill in her slender tanned hand. It was an attractive effect – very. She looked into my eyes with her blue china ones, and smiled as if I'd caught her out.

"For the sandwiches, Mr. Chesterfield," she said. "When they're ready for us."

"Mother always has a hundred handy," Carrie muttered. "Hundreds of hundreds." What the deuce was their row about?

"Don't be tacky, dear," Barbara said. "Money's a tiresome subject." As she spoke she grinned hugely at the Captain, who might have bayoneted money in the guts for tiring this great lady.

"I shall always call your handsome son 'Mr. Chesterfield'," Barbara added. "And I shall always call you 'Captain' – if that's all right."

Carrie expelled a tiny but noticeable groan.

I gave another of my little change-the-subject coughs. "So what's new since yesterday?" I said to Carrie.

Mother and daughter exchanged a glance, at which Barbara's smile froze.

"Well," Carrie said, "Larry rode on Maude. I thought that was pretty cool."

There were biggish private conversations begging to be had out all round. Yet none of them could be had out, with the gang all clotted together.

Larry was now with the shaggy bloke at the boy's laptop. I rose and went to them.

"Sorted it out, have you?" I asked.

"I think I've *figured* it out," Larry said. "But dude's in a world of hurt."

"Oh Gawd!" the shaggy boy bawled as he madly typed and clicked between websites. "There's a million charges on my credit card and nothing in my bank account!"

Hard cheese, I thought, but can we eat?

"Dude," Larry said to the panicked lad, "do you know or recognize that other kid who left, with the laptop and hat?"

The big boy's face was in his hands. "No," he moaned. "I don't know anyone else here."

"What's the matter?" Carrie called over.

"He's been evil-twinned," Larry replied. "Probably from right here in the café."

Greek it was to me, and I looked over to see Barbara Hahn and Jack Chesterfield shrugging in incomprehension. So I'm with the oldster set on this, I thought.

"What do you mean, from right here?" the young man said. "They could do it from Russia for all we know."

"But they can set you up real nice from close range," Larry said. "I say we try to catch that bearded hat kid."

With technology, I could not reason why, so I might as well do or die.

"Right," I said. "Let's after the scoundrel."

We dashed out into the street, the big boy trailing us thirtyish geezers. Larry, the boy, and I ran down separate streets, which bloomed with yuppie dog walkers, gym members, and old Italian bread ladies. But there was no hat villain. He'd got too big a start.

As I turned back towards the café, Carrie walked up to me. Again I embraced her. "Thank God we're alone a minute," I said.

She didn't catch at first that I was famished for her news. "No luck?" she said.

I took a resigned look about. "No. I mean to say, rotters need thrashing and all that, but he's not *our* rotter, is he now?"

She rested her head against my chest as I hugged her. "No, I suppose not."

"What can you tell me, love?" I probed, then to take the edge off added, "Your mum's quite marvelous with my dad, by the way."

Carrie nestled into me and, ignoring the first question, said into my chest, "Of course she is. She's furious with my father."

Aha, I thought. "This wouldn't be touching on your huge news, would it?"

Larry and the shaggy boy were trudging toward us, empty-handed.

"I don't want to tell you anymore," Carrie said almost tragically. "It could be the end of us!"

"Long gone," Larry called as he approached, with the hang-dog victim lagging after. "He looked quick like a ferret."

The big shaggy boy looked as tragic as Carrie. "My parents'll probably pull me out of school!"

I was done with this hoo-doo. I spun Carrie away from the others and back toward the café.

"Listen to me," I told her, "we're going to set a date and get ring-shopping. There is no end of us."

Finally she looked up into my eyes. Hers were liquid, tormented, and loving. "We'll have to work every day of our lives!"

"What, cut off?" I said. "So be it." As well lose two fortunes as one...

We entered the café. Barbara Hahn and Jack Chesterfield turned to us smiling, from intimate conversation. Each had a coffee going.

Barbara said across several tables, "The Captain says he may be married by tomorrow night. If certain papers get finalized!"

Well, I had signed them...

Carrie and I sat. The whole bally world was gone mad.

"Is it true, Dad?"

Captain Jack flushed. "Well," he said, "I'm just sayin', you know."

Right, I thought, and Deborah came back to mind. When you've got a fainting old man coming into millions, you don't let the grass grow...

Larry and the shaggy lad consulted at the laptop.

"Carrie, dear," her mother said. "Are you all right?"

"I'm fine, Mother," the girl said, and sniffed. "Getting married myself, you know, before long!"

"But of course you are."

Barbara Hahn, perhaps the most bewitching woman I had yet encountered, assumed for me now an almost sinister aspect... but based on bloody *what*? If the Hahns on meeting me had told their daughter, "You're cut off," Carrie would not have been so initially giddy about her huge news. Nor would Barbara be so very good to me. It was a bafflement...

And still the wrong conversations being had. Jack and Barbara were having the chin-wag of a lifetime.

"Your daughter's a gem," Captain Jack said in a tender growl. He still hardly knew his future daughter-in-law, and with Deborah on the case, he might never. Such thoughts oppressed me – after the hopes I'd had for this little brunch!

Larry rejoined us. "I'm going to bring Josh's laptop into my tech lab at school tomorrow. I won't quit till I trace it to the rat running this scam."

"Brilliant," I said, with scant interest. "I say, when's Jeanine due here?"

"One o'clock," Larry replied, and checked his watch. "Ten minutes."

I turned to Carrie. "We need more air, love, by gad we do. Let's the three of us go collect Jeanine at the gym. It's just round the corner."

I handed my father twenty dollars and bade him get whatever.

We three younger people rose again. As we slipped back out under darkening skies, young Josh was packing up his fouled laptop, while Barbara had put her hundred away.

***

No gentleman should be forever rising and sitting, coming and going. He must cultivate a steady, reassuring presence. But for myself at the café, blooming attractions, unspoken grievance, civic outrage and fear for the future were binging through the air like so many shuttlecocks that I just wanted to catch a sitter on my racket and put away one point to the good.

"All right, love," I said as we rounded the corner toward the gymnasium Ripped & Shredded. "Out with the huge news at once."

Walking in the middle of our trio, Carrie blinked at me. "In front of Larry here?"

Berkowitz trod along without reaction.

"Larry's our most trusted pal and colleague," I said. "Besides, he's mentally chasing down his cyber-Moriarty. Aren't you, mate?"

"Hm? I was just wondering what Jeanine'll be wearing."

We were one hundred yards from R & S, yet Jeanine, who must have seen us, promptly answered by popping out the gym door.

The long-slogging gentle(man) reader may even now be picturing the lovely Jeanine's lavishly inked and tautly-muscled abdomen. Such idle fantasies are of course base, and furthermore of no narrative purpose. Indeed it is a pleasure to confound class stereotype by reporting that Jeanine, just now breasting the good fresh air, wore a crisp navy nylon outer suit that was tasteful, functional, and even appropriate for what seemed an imminent shower.

Carrie and I stood like drone movie extras as this great blonde Valkyrie clinched our pal Larry in a surge of blue nylon and platinum tresses. It looked like a bit of a WWE submission hold, but the uncanny thing really was seeing Larry in the arms of a woman.

"This is Carrie," I said.

Carrie said hello.

Jeanine still held Larry like a rag doll at arms' length, and smiled ingenuously at us.

"Hel-*lo*? World's cutest couple! When ya tyin' the knot, huh?"

Larry with unaccustomed tact broke in, "Hey, since you couldn't work me out this weekend, I rode Carrie's horse."

"Omigod, that's awesome. Great for the abs and glutes!"

"Well," I said, and essayed to turn us all toward the café. "You must have seen us coming."

It was a jolly enough meet-up, but in the hundred yards to the gym I might have got the huge news. Carrie was gone silent. Dished again...

"Yeah, well," Jeanine said, "not exactly my favorite people in the house today, no offense. I thought I'd spare everybody, and myself."

Say again? I looked back at the street by the gym and saw Deborah's car out front. And there was a monstrous super-sled hulking nearby, a kind of mega-SUV that would dwarf even Barbara Hahn's Range Rover. Vanity plate saying... well, the especially acute long-slogging reader will have it: LOCK IN.

Right. "You three go on," I said. "I'll just have a look-in."

Ripped & Shredded, minus the good cheer of Jeanine, was now a wasteland sort of place. You did not see regular folks sweating off those stubborn twenty on treadmills and such. Instead, I noted as I slipped into its eerie quiet, the gym was half full with hyper-muscled males between twenty and forty, and a few women less massive but no less "cut." Most denizens, male and female, seemed in solitary worlds of their own, except for a few "spotting" each other on bars laden with iron plates.

Where was Deborah in all this? Nowhere that I could see.

At the front desk was a young male typical of the larger crowd: head shaved (no body hair either), dressed in a singlet with tanned muscles bulging. He looked up unsmiling at me.

"Help you?"

"I shan't trouble you," I replied. "Just looking in on a friend. Good old Benedict Hoepplewhite back as a member these days?"

The young man studied me for irony, for motive. "He's the owner now."

"Oh, I say."

Upon this utterance I saw a film of hostility cloud the young man's eyes. I had lately been round such decent folk that I'd forgot there were people who could loathe and distrust me for my diction alone.

"Anything else?" the young man said.

"I guess not," I said, scanning the main floor again. "I don't see him about."

The young man, had he proper manners, might have offered something helpful. Instead he said, "You won't. He's got trainers for the floor."

I made a lean toward the front, to reduce the tension. "Ah, right. The lovely Jeanine, et al."

The young man just looked at me through that film of enmity.

"Well," I said, "must be going. Good to know friend Hoepplewhite's back in the chips again."

The young man might have asked who was well-wishing his boss, but didn't.

Still no sign of Deborah as I eased to the door. Across the vast gym floor, though, an office door opened. Through it stepped a figure as out of place here as myself.

It was that goateed young devil in the fedora. Under one arm he still carried his laptop. The opposite hand was held to his face as if he'd been struck.

The young man went from the office door through another door. But it was all interior. After exiting the gym and standing several minutes' watch, I never saw the boy re-emerge.

***

Back at the café, I found Barbara Hahn directly leaving for home. Jack Chesterfield stood gallantly. Larry and Jeanine sat with new big salads. Carrie just stood.

"Madame," I said, "let me take Carrie as well as my father home. You can easily hit the interstate spur just up the street from here."

Mother, daughter, future son-in-law looked flurriedly each to each, as if all was unfinished. But Barbara did her first duty, which was to pull Carrie to her and kiss her on both cheeks.

"Darling daughter, how blessed you are. Your parents love you, and so does Mr. Chesterfield!"

Whatever her grievance, Carrie could not complain of this. And she did not. More importantly, my deepest intuition told me it was far, far better to see full-throated love from the mother, and pique in the daughter, than the reverse. Thus all was well, if not perfect. And if it were only about money, then nothing really was wrong at all.

THE WRONG WHISKY

Later that night, my father and I sat in the den of my house. A bottle of twelve year-old single malt scotch, with cut-glass ice bucket, stood on a small table between us. Through the screen windows came the pleasant sound and breeze of late June rain. Each of us had a scotch rocks going.

Jack sipped, then lowered his glass. "By God, this is the best I've ever had."

"Quite," I said. "Thanks for bringing."

"Your mother gave it to me last Christmas, and I haven't had occasion to break it out."

"Her funeral after-gathering might have done," I said. "Oh, right, there never was one."

In the corner of my eye I saw the guv'nor's head turn toward me.

"We'll need to have a memorial service, of course," Jack said.

"Good of you to say so, Dad. But first your bachelor party, if that's what this is."

Deborah's selective ceremoniousness had her out to dinner and a movie with her girlfriends, so Jack wouldn't see her this night. In fact they'd spoken only by phone all day. There is perhaps a virginal June wedding charm to such superstitious separation. Perhaps there isn't...

"Don't be that way, son," Jack said. "Your mother just... went away. Nothing's real anymore."

I drank and held the really very fine whisky in my mouth a moment. Then I swallowed and said, "Deborah once was quite real to me. Now she'll be your reality, tomorrow and tomorrow."

"Right," Jack said, as if accepting sentence.

"I'm going straight back out of town tomorrow, so I can't be best-manning it for you. I wouldn't anyway."

"Back to those lakes, eh?" Jack said, and with an audible gulp emptied his glass. "I almost envy you."

The best whiskies induce an overall bodily fine feeling. I felt as one with my favorite chair...

"Ah," I said, waving my drink a bit now. "Madame Hahn and all that. She's gone away too, hey Dad? Never real."

"I hope not," Jack said, fumbling now for new ice, which in fact was quite old ice and mostly water. "I mean I hope she's real. For you."

"Well, that's the way it's got to be, init?" I felt a goodish warmth now.

Jack took a pull on his new drink. "What way?" he said.

"Well, of course, I mean no Barbara for you, old buffer, and no dad-in-law for my Carrie. I mean to say, poor though I'll be, I'll still be having these wonderful in-laws, but my little Carrie won't have a father-in-law, because your new boss, this Deborah person, will be having none of it, d'you see? Well done, I say!"

I reached for the bottle, and as the ice in the bucket was fast melting, poured myself two fingers of the straight stuff.

Jack Chesterfield sat stoically holding his glass, staring forward. Daisy slept on the rug across from us, enjoying the gentle moist breeze. The room, with just one floor lamp on, had darkened. Addled as I was, it could have been three hours either side of midnight. There was no knowing...

As soon as the fresh, double-strong scotch hit my tongue, I recoiled as if burnt.

"Good God! Where's that bloody ice?" I reached for the bucket.

"Hanh?" Jack said as if waked.

"Ice, I say. Is there a solid piece in this whole puke pot... my mouth's on fire... give me ice... "

Tink-a-link...

a-dink...

"What ho, you men," the voice said from a darkened corner by the window curtains. "Safe to say you're off parade?"

Captain Jack bolted up with a gulping sort of a half-snore. Daisy had awakened and stared intently toward the form by the curtains.

Though less surprised, I must say I sobered instantly.

"What ho, Mother. You're back from the lakes."

The old bluish figure assumed some form: the face indistinct, the Manhattan glass sharply defined at the end of a ghostly clothed arm.

"Daphne!" Jack said. "Are you trying to kill me?"

The glass moved upward to the shadowy face. The ancient ring glittered. The ice clinked as she sipped.

"Oh, do buck up. Did I really marry such a fainting ponce?"

"Please, Mother," I said. "You needn't go for him baldheaded like that."

"I suppose," Daphne said. "What's that rotgut swill you're having, anyway?"

"Only your last gift to him in this world, Mother. But it's nothing."

"By God," Jack said, "when sex and whisky have me seeing monsters, my life as a man is over."

"Monster! I like that for bloody cheek." She sipped again. "Anyway, your life as a man *is* over, but don't blame little me."

As she said this, I remembered how I'd blearily awoken that morning with two realizations. The first, previously related, was that I missed my mother, her actual living presence and touch, her badinage, too, with my father.

The second realization, call it bone-deep conviction, was that The Fortune in fact *did not* exist...

The phone rang in the kitchen, with such shocking clangor that I feared I'd been electrocuted in my favorite lounging chair.

"Who the hell can that be at this hour?" my father bellowed almost in terror.

"Oh, shut up, Jack," my mother said. "As if it were your house!"

I wobbled to my feet. "You two have your argy-bargy," I said. "I'm going to take that."

The bright overhead kitchen light blasted my eyes. More shocking yet was the clock saying just 9:35. I flicked the lights off and took up the phone. It was Carrie.

"I must have seemed a terrible brat today," she said.

"Never, love, ever."

"No no, I was, but I want you to know I heard what you said outside the café, and I return your devotion. There is no end of us."

"Then this huge news of yours doesn't dish us after all?"

I heard her take a big breath and sigh it out. "It just means I'm land-poor, that's all. Father's deeding me the entire estate, all the way down to the lake, effective this week."

So much for being cut off. Snoggered, sobered-up, haunted, electrocuted and blinded all in just the past few minutes, I did my level damnedest to take it coolly.

"Land-poor's a solecism, I think, love. Land-rich and cash-poor, perhaps. I'd say the whole boodle probably cuts up at about five million." I'd after all been casing Canandaigua rents and real estate.

"But Father insists I lease him the commercial rights to the vineyards and stables, so he can go on minting money from his grapes and winery and horses. He'll pay me a dollar a year – and the taxes are thirty-thousand!"

"And your mother? Cut out entirely, then?"

"Oh," Carrie said with a slight waver, "no violins for Mother. Father will be slipping her the same fistfuls of cash he always has. She has buckets."

"Ah. Still, she might feel a tad dispossessed. Why's your father doing this?"

"Because of you."

"I beg your pardon?"

"He likes you. He thinks you're probably a good guy, but since you've got nothing he's taking no chances. The estate's always been in his sole name, and now it's going to be in mine, in case you turn out to be a... a... what would *you* call it?"

"A bounder."

"Right, a bounder. Father would *love* to have that in his vocabulary, but it doesn't come to him."

"Well," I said, "he's got *gonif*, but won't use it. Listen, love, I'm off to Canandaigua tomorrow, to find digs and work. I shan't trouble your folks."

"You won't. They're coming down *here* to move me home. I've got to be out of my flat by June 30."

"Then you're ready to take possession – Lady Hahn-Chesterfield!"

"I'll be working at Burger King to pay the taxes!"

"I'll do my part, love, really I will. Though to say I've got *nothing* is a bit thick."

***

I returned to the den to find my father asleep and my mother gone. Daisy looked up at me from the rug.

Drunk is drunk, and so were I and my father, so the son would have to put the father to bed here. First, some clearing off...

No sooner had I capped the whisky bottle than something caught my eye, from inside my guv'nor's glass. It was the gold ring, a century and a half old, encrusted with diamonds and sapphires: the only thing of great value Daphne Ffoulkes Chesterfield claimed ever to have owned.

I shook the whisky and water off it, and pocketed it. This might do something, I thought, as the villain Iago said of Desdemona's handkerchief.

But it would not do wickedness. Being in my father's glass, it was my father's ring – that's the way I saw it. And if the ring ended on Deborah's finger, then it was meant to be and thus no wickedness. In the morning it would go to Captain Jack.

It is tedious and exhausting to do chores late at night with a whisky head. But I put the dishes away and fixed Daisy with fresh food and water. Then to my father – I will spare the poor reader, who has ample imagination to do the filling for us. Then to bed...

"Blimey, dear, how you've foxed them!"

Daphne had left, but her voice, as it recurred for the second straight night in my dreams, was from earlier in the spring.

Foxed them how? By blessing Jack and Deborah's ménage, throwing them The Fortune as the base Judean threw a pearl away, to be with my own true love? A biggish price to pay...

Not too big for me, loving Carrie as I did, but a different kettle of kippers for Daphne, who'd lived so long betrayed and pension-bound. No, my mother's ghost had put it to me pretty straight, if only I'd been ready to hear it. There was no Fortune.

Unless it was the lovely little ring, and if that went to Deborah for all her years of grailing, I wouldn't give it another thought in this world.

END BOOK THREE, PART TWO

Part Three

RING CEREMONY

In the early morning, a realtor of Deborah's choosing hammered a For Sale sign into the lawn of our Cape Cod. It was, as has been noted, a boom time for housing, and in decent metropolitan neighborhoods one could expect a quick and profitable sale.

I certainly hoped so, for my and Carrie's sake. There was a mortgage to retire, and then the fifty-fifty split with Deborah, but even after all that I'd be taking a fair nest-egg to a cheaper town. That is to say that charming Canandaigua, apart from lofty West Lake Road, was a blooming bargain. I just might get a real house there with the Cape Cod's crumbs.

Or I could rent. Though this narrative couldn't possibly have any sub-prime gentle readers, even solider sorts may look back from our present post-apocalypse and wonder: What if I had only... ?

Well, that's what my second trip was about. Certainly I would not presume to move in at the Hahns', er, at Carrie's West Lake Road estate. I would make my own way.

My father was up early as well, and displayed no signs of head. I went to him directly with Daphne's ring.

I gently rapped on the open door to the guest room. Captain Jack, standing next the bed, first looked me in the eye, then dropped his gaze to the sparkling object in my hands.

This day, Monday, at City Hall or some such municipal rat-trap, my divorce would take effect. It will already have occurred to legion readers and been universally acknowledged that a single man of no fortune should be in want of a ring. Especially a free one. But no matter...

"Take this, Dad. Do with it what you will."

My old man took the ring, more to wonder at than to possess it. His eyes welled.

"The reading of the will is this coming Friday," he offered out of the clear blue.

"Ah."

This impenetrable response of mine, which after all was the mere habit of the gentleman, seemed to further animate my guv'nor, who'd been equally reticent on this immense and sticky subject. A Marine, after all, is a sort of a gentleman.

"You'll be there, won't you?" Jack said, still with strange emotion. Perhaps it tingled in the fingers that held the ring, traveled up through the heart, the voice, out the eyes which leaked...

"I could be," I said. "Do I need to be?"

"I'd like to have you!"

"But will Deborah?"

Involuntarily Jack Chesterfield looked down at the little ring, which seemed almost a single gem in his big hands.

"We don't know if Daphne'd want me to have this," he said. "Maybe you're the guy for it, huh?"

"I'm not," I said. "You're the guy all right. As to whether Deborah's the girl for it, neither Mother nor I could possibly say. Only you can now."

"Okay," the Captain said, and put the ring in his pocket. His face drooped with that absence of certitude which is death for a soldier. "Maybe the will's got something to say about it."

I was doubly ready to get out of town now.

"The will won't, so again I say, do with the ring what you will. Perhaps it showed up right on time. All best of luck tonight."

I turned on my heel and walked out. Within fifteen minutes I'd chowed down, grabbed my bag, got in the car with Daisy, and left for the lake country.

THE CHESTERFIELD HOURS

THE CHOSEN SPOT

At ten o'clock that night, I lay reading on my bed in a cheapish motel that allowed pets. Daisy slept against my legs. Together we'd done a great deal of walking round Canandaigua town. We'd seen the vibrant, chain-free downtown of small businesses, pitched on the hill swooping down to the lake. Further up North Main was the Preservation District, mansions a bit over my means, which also included St. John's Episcopal and all the major churches. At the east border of the District were the spectacular Sonnenberg Mansion and Gardens, which would have done Queen Victoria proud. Indeed, the old statues, the domed greenhouses, the chipped walkways and untrimmed weeping willows, the ochre ponds pulled one through the looking glass back to a less manicured yet lovelier time.

I'd stopped into a realtor's office on South Main, the lake in view, and got the lowdown on houses priced between one and two hundred thousand. Daisy's being leashed to the realtor's porch railing helped keep the sales chat short, and I left with a print-out.

I knew I wanted to live in town. Of course one could fantasize commanding the West Lake Road estate, but however it was deeded, in my mind it was Shemp and Barbara Hahn's place. I had long lived at least putatively as master of my house, and could never stick it as an in-law hanger-on, with Shemp commenting on my every "wardrobe change."

The charm of the town, were I to buy affordably just off the District, was that I could walk to church, to downtown, to the YMCA, to City Hall, even to the bluesilver lake. There was also a flat for rent above a picture framer in the South Main business district. I would interview the owner for his pets policy and general worldview.

Right. And I had visited the booming Finger Lakes Community College and learned they needed adjuncts.

Of course, adjunct teachers are not the lads and lassies for tackling thirty-thousand dollar tax bills. Still, it had been a productive afternoon after a long drive up, and now I lay dozily turning a last page...

The ancient motel phone went off beside me like an air-raid siren.

As I picked up I felt so disordered I imagined my mother on the other end, inquiring whether this dive motel was fit for the well-bred ghost to visit...

Instead it was Larry Berkowitz.

"Oh, hallo, old fish. Say, Carrie was awfully glad to meet Jeanine – she was just so wrapped up with her mother we couldn't properly -- "

"It's fine, Chest, don't worry about it. I'm calling about the evil-twin scam. I cracked it."

"Brilliant lad! Tell it me as if to a child." I was wide-awake now, in fact feeling the good old adrenaline surge of battle call. Why would that be?

"It's big," Larry said. "It's nation-wide, in fact, maybe world-wide. Yet it's based locally."

"I see," I said casually as I could. "Operating out of the Ripped & Shredded gymnasium."

Larry paused a moment. "What were you thinking when you went back there yesterday?"

"That Hoepplewhite and Deborah had returned as members. I learned instead that he's the owner now. And that little laptop beatnik in the fedora was there."

"Has it occurred to you," Larry said, "that when we tried that Super Bowl sting on Hoepplewhite, we may have awakened him to, quote unquote, the power of the Internet?"

I did not want to think it. "What exactly are those devils up to?"

"Hoepplewhite's got these hacker punks working college towns across the country, wi-fi joints like our café, full of idiot rich kids. Evil-twinning 'em and stealing from accounts, basically."

"Right," I gritted out, remembering Hoepplewhite's bottomless amoral hoggishness. "He entereth the sheepfold not by the gate. The worm-guts toad."

"Money's funneling into our local bank, the same one our school district uses. No way I'm gonna hack in there to find out how much, but it's got to be millions and millions."

"Good God! Hoepplewhite the Meyer Lansky of the Millennium."

"Well, anyway that's the scheme. How's the apartment hunting?" Larry, who was scared of Deborah, assumed she would leave me scrounging for poorhouse digs.

"A fair start," I replied. "But after what you've told me I'm coming home directly tomorrow – to pay a call on friend Hoepplewhite."

"Think twice."

"Say again?"

"Well," Larry said, "Jeanine says the place reeks of steroids. They sell it in the locker rooms, the members all juice up, high school kids come in to buy it. Blech."

"Despicable," I said. "But let's stick to the larger felony for now, shall we?"

"Yeah, except... "

"Yes, mate?"

Larry let out a breath. "Don't go up against him, Chest. Hoepplewhite's roided up himself now, big-time. Since we... since he got busted up, Jeanine says he trains from six to eight every morning, then disappears into his office."

"There to run his evil empire. But he'll not fence me out."

"She says you wouldn't recognize him, he's a hulk now. She wants to quit, he pushes them around so bad. But what can she do? She's got no degree."

A flood of guilt and remorse washed over me. The long-slogging reader will have a good idea why. It is one thing to pimp one's wife to one's father – that one seemed to have struck the right note – but quite another to put the fair Jeanine in this Hoepple'roid's path... as I had carelessly done, away back in the winter...

"Don't worry, old man," I told Larry in my nonchalantest tone. "I have always dominated Hoepplewhite. I've got the blighter easy-peasy."

THE CHESTERFIELD HOURS

AT THE VIOLENT HOUR

A youngish man in love both throbs and waits -- but like Eliot's taxi, this human engine only waits to go, to go, to go...

Yet I, after four three-hundred mile car trips in five days, was going nowhere – except straightaway to a crack-up.

Too much disconnection was doing it. Not plugs and wires, if we can now and hereafter garage the man-as-machine metaphor.

No, the human connections, so ethereal yet so crucial, were all knotted, severed, askew, unnatural. I was going crackers because Carrie hadn't been with me in any real way since we'd messily clinched Friday night at her parents'; going crackers because Hoepplewhite had resurged, Hoepplewhite who'd been amusing as a kind of booby squire/Malvolio/comic villain sort, but who now bulked something vastly more sinister...

Crackers because my father would be married now, the family ring on Deborah's finger. And now how ugly might the estate settlement get, three days hence, should Daphne's worldly goods amount to a mere frock or two...

Chugging yet again back into the metrop from Canandaigua, I drove by Ripped & Shredded. Hoepplewhite's hippo of an SUV was not there. Perhaps, if the villain came in at six, he was out by three. It was already past four.

THE CHESTERFIELD HOURS

I drove next past Carrie's flat, which showed some life. Her little car was there, and Barbara's Range Rover, and a pick-up truck with a trailer hitched to it. The sight stabbed at me. My girl was really going. I must do the same, but that was another human thread gone dicky. My girl was now "land-poor", which is to say rich. I was just plain poor. Carrie would say it didn't matter... human history says otherwise...

Impotent anger, or fear, or guilt (Jeanine!) of course are notorious toxins. At least I'd had Daisy beside me to stroke and talk to during the drive. Now home...

Whereas last homecoming I'd been distracted by Barbara Hahn, this time I looked straight to the telephone, which flashed messages. I punched...

A strange voice said our house had sold. Was it possible? If someone had met our listing price, it was done.

So I'd soon have money, some anyway. Deborah would too, but what was that against her grievance, should The Fortune prove a fable? Friday's estate settlement now overwhelmed my imagination. There was no Fortune. What would that do to Deborah, and what would she do to Captain Jack?

My father had left a message also. His voice said, "Son, I -- "

-- but I punched the Save button

I fixed Daisy fresh food and water and set off for the shopping mall.

**

Soon I was looking at diamond rings. Mall jewelers are not the first choice of the gentleman, unless he's gone dotty crackers. My legs and spirit were heavy with travel, lack of food, and foreboding – yet the day and situation wanted action.

237

I saw one I liked. What the deuce did I know of gems? Daphne's ring with its diamonds and sapphires was my ideal -- but they weren't making more of them. The saleswoman showed me a blow-up of my chosen one, for its alleged clarity. It could have been a shite carbuncle for all my present judgment...

"I'll take it," I said, and pulled my credit card. The only thing for it is to act, I told myself, against voices chanting in my head like the Weird Sisters.

As the saleswoman put it through, I walked a taut circle. The place smelled of Windex; all day they must be wiping grimy fingerprints from the panels of glass...

"I'm sorry, sir, it's been declined. The ring's over your credit limit."

"But it's the one I want!"

She was an elegant forty-something in a grey suit and white blouse, her hair in a butterscotch Cinnabon. A niceish lady...

"Perhaps you'd care to make a down-payment today?"

"I... I really need the whole ring today!"

She smiled. Perhaps she'd thought the flustered groom had gone the way of the dodo, replaced by bullying tossers who "want what they want."

"We'll make sure you never get less than the whole ring," she said. "Promise!"

I felt blood surge to my face, then wash back out, leaving me chalkish and weak-kneed.

"Dreadfully sorry. Another time, perhaps." At that I fled the mall.

***

I drove past Carrie's again, though I had nothing to give her. But I needed her voice, her touch – perhaps they were all I needed to come back to myself again. For days there'd been worlds of people put between us...

Her car was not there, but the Range Rover, pick-up and trailer were. Cyrus barked and ran to the door as I stepped onto the porch.

"Why, Mr. Chesterfield!" Barbara Hahn exclaimed upon opening to me. "I'd thought you were in New York."

She wore a pink button-down oxford shirt, Brooks Brothers probably, with faded jeans and white sneakers. The mane of hair was pulled back in her "working" ponytail.

"Just back," I said. "I... I've been missing Carrie awfully, madame. Can't seem to connect."

Barbara Hahn took both my hands in hers. I looked down and studied hers. She had a wedding band and a large diamond ring on the left ring finger – nothing on the other nine. I had felt the big sparkler knock against my hand each time she took it in this way of hers. It was rousing and disconcerting both. I imagined Daphne's ring on Barbara; it had just her colors, more so than green-eyed Carrie's...

"Oh, you've just missed her," Barbara said. "Shemp wanted Chinese food after all our packing, and he and Carrie went off to get some."

Even my own mother's ghost, I felt, had left me in the lurch. I held to Barbara's hands, and hung on her voice for a needy moment... but it were weakness and sloth to do so...

"Well," I said, snapping to, "barging in like this is not the done thing. I've badly let drop the mask, and beg your pardon."

She pulled up my hands and held them against her breastbone. Her blue china eyes devoured mine with less merriment but no less sympathy than before.

"Wear the mask too long, and the face grows to fit it. How is your dear father? On his honeymoon?"

Thoughts of this other thread appalled me, as they had when I'd stopped Jack's message.

"I don't seem to know where anyone is, madame," I said, and gave back her delicious hands. "I'm really not anywhere myself."

I retreated to the car and directly drove away. I needed to see my Carrie, but did not need to see her with Shemp and his oozing white take-out boxes.

***

No honeymoon for Jack and Deborah. It was a Tuesday, for God's sake. They'd have done the dismal ceremony in a darkened deserted office, and probably Deborah had gone right to work today...

No honeymoon for now, when they could throw a big blow-out in the fall, populated with hairless, muscled-up young gym addicts, aliens to my father...

No honeymoon yet, because for Deborah the real ceremony was this coming Friday, at the estate reading...

That thread wouldn't bear further tugging. Only to say they weren't honeymooning, that Deborah would have worked, and it was now past quitting time...

...thus she might be at the gym. I veered from the street that led home. Just a quick curious last look at Ripped & Shredded...

Her car was not there. Hoepplewhite's grotesque thing was, however.

What if I had a cell phone, like everyone bloody else? Right, I'd be awash in the world's anecdotal drivel. Yet I'd also know what had happened, and hadn't...

No matter. I swung my Honda in behind Hoepplewhite's great hippo-wagon. On entering, I didn't trifle with the arrogant hairless lad at the desk. I drifted on by...

The words "Help you?" fell away behind me. Because of my apparent innocuous aimlessness I was not pursued. Other varied human types were looking out upon the great gym floor – why not myself?

I spied Jeanine out on the floor, sweeping the floor between Stairmaster machines. This, though doubtless a small part of her duties, struck a plangent chord in me. I approached her. As I did, I looked to the door of the big office, which displayed not Hoepplewhite's name but simply "Private."

Jeanine had a red shiny welt on her left cheekbone. It was no black eye, rather a sick mockery of an apple cheek.

She spotted me. "Hey, Chest!" she said with a spontaneous warm smile, and then with a heartbreaking self-conscious afterthought raised a hand to her cheek.

I took her hand. "Are you quite all right?"

I'd never seen her happy eyes cloud before – but I hadn't known her, not really...

"I'm ... what the heck ya doin' here, huh?"

I recalled the fedora lad fleeing that office, a hand pressed to his face. I turned from Jeanine toward the door. The knob would not turn.

Yes, I'd felt weakish all afternoon. Not now. How dare this imbecile door be locked? With a thrust from coiled legs, I drove my shoulder into the door and splintered the lock.

The whole building seemed screaming. Two weird figures bent before me in an obscene *danse macabre*. A vaster Hoepplewhite than I'd ever imagined goggled my disbelieving eyes. There was a stick figure almost on top of him, that of the goateed lad, minus hat. Hoepplewhite's pants were down and a great long needle jutted from his bum, as the boy plunged the muscle-building filth into him.

"What the f--- !"

Hoepplewhite straightened, his great veinous muscles fluttering. While his rear end stuck out that lurid needle, his nether front was nearly not there at all. Oh, call it a button and be charitable. There is a heavy price to pay to get such muscles, and here was graphic proof of robbing peter...

"Your swords I smile at," I said. "Put up your pants and fight!"

Hoepplewhite plucked the needle himself and threw it to the floor. Then he shoved the goateed lad toward me, roaring, "Get him the f--- out of here!"

The slight spidery boy wavered timorously in my path. With one arm I swept him away like dry bones, and the boy just disappeared.

I advanced on the foe. "Eternal villain, now do I meet you beard to beard, and beat you backwards home."

Those who never step into the arena might scoff that muscle gained from steroids is not "real." I, with time for reflection, might have argued the point. But I was busy, after a brief clinch, whizzing through the air and into the wall, where something crunched and sent a shock of pain through one shoulder. My head, too, went woozy.

But groggily sprawled as I was, I saw flashing the arrow of God, in the form of a blue-suited, platinum-headed girl. Jeanine, with a great avenging cry, darted at Hoepplewhite...

"Aaaiiiargh!"

It takes main strength, not steroidal bulk, to grip and hold fast a wee small object. Plumbers have such strength, and mechanics. Coming back to my senses, essaying to stand, I saw Jeanine seize and drag the screaming Hoepplewhite by yon fleshy nubbin, out into the main room where she threw him to the mat. Certainly the throwing, by such a sensitive lever, had properly finished him.

Jeanine had already got 911 on her cell phone when the hairless front-desk knob-head walked up with his arms spread, bellowing in suburban gangsterese, "Whassup witchou, b---- ?"

An onerous customer he seemed, and to meet in any sense beard to beard with him might go hardly for Jeanine. But as he acted so confident of cowing her with voice alone, and because he multiplied the force of her right-hand punch by walking arrogantly straight into it, that punch sent him directly off to dreamland. Rockabye baby...

I had staggered out into this end-scene. Pain knifed me between neck and shoulder. Something was broken, but not my head at least. Jeanine, with the two villains stretched out at her feet, spoke into her phone.

"Yeah, Ripped & Shredded on P____ Street. Get right over here." She snapped the phone shut.

I should not have stood. My legs were going again. Yet I felt exultant, lighter. Also I felt tender, absolved. Jeanine had a hand under my back. I lightly touched the welt on her cheek...

"Easy, Chest," she was saying as she lowered me. "Just relax and trust me here."

Next I was on a soft mat Jeanine had jerked out from under Hoepplewhite. I might have quibbled at lying with scoundrels, but as I faded to black I was rising to the angels.

THE RING OF TRUTH

Larry Berkowitz was first into the hospital to visit me. Jeanine didn't even know Carrie's last name, much less her number. But Larry on the way had called the flat and caught her still eating with her parents.

"I'm glad to have you alone, old fish, before the hordes arrive." I lay on my back with my head propped, broken clavicle set but throbbing.

"The cops found a ton of steroids at the gym," Larry said. "Of course, Jeanine will get dragged into that, and the evil-twin case will be complicated by the moronic shtunk you made."

"Did you bring me anything?" I said. "I've hardly eaten all day."

"No food for you. Do you realize you took the absolute stupidest course of action?"

"Maybe if I'd had something to eat first. Look here, old man, I want to talk to you."

Larry paused in his pacing. "Oh, *you* want to talk to *me*? That's a good one. Do you also realize Jeanine's out of a job?"

"So am I, so's Carrie, so's everyone but you. In fact, you're on a brilliant trajectory now, mate. But will you seize the day?"

Larry with his nervous energy had got pacing again, but yet again pulled up short and stared at me.

"Hah?"

I ticked off points with my good hand and arm.

"Only think of where you've come since ringing in the New Year as a certified non-entity. In winter you had a fake dinner date with a real girl, during which you fake knocked me out. In spring you had your first love affair, putridly sordid though it was. By June you had vanquished, hand to hand, a large sixth grader. At school year's end, you became a tenured professional. Recent unconfirmed reports have you riding a horse. And now you have cracked a world-wide scheme to defraud millions."

"You've done a lot for me, Chest. Not lately, though."

"You ass, I could never better stead thee than now. Must I draw you pictures of how to build on this?"

"Forget it," Larry said. "I called in the FBI, so they'll get the credit."

"Nonsense. You could land a book deal for your part in it."

"Except I can't write."

"I was rather counting on that," I said, "being in want of a job. Which brings me back to Jeanine."

"What about her?"

I pounced. "Yes, what about her? If you're fully a man now, you'll directly propose to her."

Those dratted eyebrows bunched. "Already?"

I myself never blinked. "This night. She's a dead-game filly, none better."

Larry looked at me wonderingly. "But -- "

"Chuck the tedious courtship charade: first coffee, then dinner, next the cheek bloody kiss, the mouth bloody kiss, meet the bloody parents, next get the undies off her... bollocks the whole load of rubbish! Go straight to her now."

Exhausted from this peroration, I settled back on my pillow and turned away. "Go and do your duty."

There were little footsteps in the hall, approaching. Carrie appeared in the door just as Larry walked to it.

"Do come in, love," I said. "Larry's just leaving."

Carrie and Larry exchanged looks and shrugged at each other. Then Larry slipped away.

Carrie took a tentative step further in. "What's the matter with him?"

I drank in the sight of her, in tee shirt, jeans and sneakers. She looked harder-worked than had her mother, which was proper.

"There's not a thing the matter with him," I said. "Like Hemingway's younger waiter, he has youth, confidence, and a job. He has everything."

She came to my side and took my hand. "And then there's you."

"Right," I said, and kissed her hand. "Feeling a bit older-waiterish. It all seemed to go wrong when I went ring-shopping."

With an in-rush of breath she swooped down at me. I felt her breasts on my ribs, but thoughtfully she stayed off my bad side. We kissed.

"You promised we'd ring-shop together!" she scolded, but clearly my "badness" warmed her. I encircled her waist with my good right arm.

"I know," I said. "It was bad karma, or something, to go without you."

"You enormous idiot," she further scolded as she nuzzled me, "fighting with Hoepplewhite. You should have let me call Dominic."

"What, mobsters on speed dial?" I said. "The girl I'm going to marry!"

"At number six, God! Totally behind you, my parents, Larry, and somebody I can't remember."

I kissed her darling little ear. "You totally shouldn't say 'totally.'"

She was squatting and reaching rather awkwardly so we could touch without hurting me. I had gone days without even hand-holding, without private words and endearments.

"I say, love, have we not been massively chaste down all the days?"

She rubbed a hand in circles along my chest, short of the collarbone. "Tot... oh, massively, yes."

"And I a single man now," I said, rubbing her hand which rubbed me.

She pulled back wide-eyed and gave a little gasp. "Oh my God, that's right!"

"Right," I said, my hand in her hair, pulling her face back toward me. "Now I fully expect that we as gentlefolk will go the distance."

"Will we?" she said, rubbing wider circles.

I, feeling warmish, paused to breathe.

"Isn't it awkward, love, your having to kneel or squat? Do climb on and we'll properly cuddle. Just stay off my hot spot."

"Which one?"

She climbed aboard and, petite as she was, lay along my good right side.

"Patience, children," Barbara Hahn said from the doorway. "A fall wedding's the earliest we can decently do."

"Mother! You've been listening."

"No," Barbara said as she entered carrying a stack of magazines, "watching. Was there something to hear?"

"Do come in, madame," I said.

"I am in, Mr. Chesterfield." As she placed the magazines on a table, Barbara showed her arresting gapped smile. "Yet I'm never sure whether I'm one beat late or right on time."

"Because you never ask," Carrie said.

"Please forgive me, madame. I've never before failed to rise upon your appearance."

"You've still not failed by my lights, dear boy," she said, looking me up and down. "Carrie of course is helpful in her way."

"Mother!"

I was aware again of being five degrees too warm. "I feel terribly that your dinner was disturbed," I said.

"Father sends his best," Barbara said. "He's so thrilled to find the Mets game broadcast in your city."

"Right," I mumbled. "Sixty games a year on basic cable, the rest if you buy the package."

Carrie had resumed rubbing chest circles, little six-inch innocent ones. As I gazed at Barbara Hahn, Jack Chesterfield suddenly appeared over her shoulder.

"Dad! How'd you know?"

"I called him, Mr. Chesterfield," Barbara said. "Risking the ire of the new bride!"

She turned smiling to Jack, but this time withheld her familiar hand. "You really are torn in your duties, Captain."

Like a private caught loafing, Carrie leapt from the bed, to something like attention. She and my dad looked at each other like the near-strangers they were.

"No," Jack said, "my duties are here." He fished in his pocket.

"Deborah would argue the point," I said.

The guv'nor had reddened. "Deborah would argue any point." He paused to sigh. "We're not married."

I heard the Hahn women each expel something, but only Jack's reverberating utterance seemed to register. Then my father spoke to Carrie, with a kind of wonderment.

"You're going to be my daughter-in-law."

She seemed amazed to be addressed by him.

"Yes," was all she said. At the café she had seen the Captain's gaze go always to her mother. Not now.

Jack had something in his hand. "My son told me the other night that I'd be strangers to you and your moth... to you and your parents, if I married Deborah."

"Oh, Captain," Barbara Hahn said, "Young Mr. Chesterfield was too hard on you." Now she felt free to take him by hand.

Jack might have loved as ever this feline stroking, yet something kept his eyes on the daughter.

"My son also gave me this the other night." He produced the gold ring with its diamonds and sapphires.

The women gasped.

"Dad, no," I said. "I'm buying Carrie her own ring. That's *my* duty."

"Well, what the hell use have I got for it now?" Jack asked.

His anguished eyes swept across us other three, then fastened on me. "I couldn't give Daphne's ring to Deborah. And if I couldn't do that, I couldn't marry her."

"Ah," I said, "so it's Mother's fault."

Another terrific shift of emotion, as of seeing a ghost, crossed the old man's face.

"Yes, God bless her! Because I'd have taken our family to the dogs!" He held the ring out to Carrie, who looked to me, her hands still at her sides.

"Put it away, Dad, and give it to your next wife. Carrie can have it when you both are dead, and when Carrie's dead it'll go to our daughter, or to our son's wife if she's worthy."

The brutality of this pronouncement seemed almost to thrill the room. What is dynasty without death? Carrie hugged Jack, while Barbara wrapped his fingers fast round the ring, then guided the hand into his pocket.

"We all must husband our treasures, Captain," Barbara said. "Good news! Your excellent son says you *will* marry again, more appropriately and propitiously. And your late good wife is immortalized."

"Is she ever," I said, at which the guv'nor shot me a look. "You know, Dad, even Deborah mightn't repine after Friday, when The Fortune proves a fiction."

"Oh, that." Jack seemed embarrassed by the subject. "I told her she could come to the reading – she wants to know how it comes out."

"What? And you too guilty to say no?"

Jack looked in appeal to Carrie and Barbara, and shrugged haplessly.

"Well, I promised," was all he said.

"Why, she'll rail in the streets. Madame, am I too apocalyptic?"

"Well," Barbara said, "*I* wouldn't rail, but then I wouldn't have bungled it as she has."

"Oh," Carrie blurted, "Deborah's a... a... I don't know!"

"Right, love, you don't know."

I reached out for her again, and she bent to my kiss, her expression still clouded.

"All will be well. Friday you'll be in the Finger Lakes, on your magnificent estate with your beloved parents and animals."

She pulled back and wiggled her ring finger at me. "And what will you be doing?"

I lay back on the pillow and shut my eyes. "Well, I'm going to have to attend that estate reading. Won't I now?"

SWIFT DISPATCH

Friday morning broke sunny and crisp for early summer. The rainy spell had passed, blown away by a drying cold front. This freshening, too, would ripen and burst, by the end of the holiday weekend just now beginning. The reading of Daphne Ffoulkes Chesterfield's will was at seven that evening, in a downtown skyscraper office.

The immensity of Fourth of July in this city felt equally before and behind me. Carrie was gone to the lakes with her parents, her stuff, and Cyrus. I wasn't sure where I'd be come Monday, but I knew I was moving on. I'd sent my notice to the school district, a biggish life crossing. I was all in now...

But I had been all in, really, since I'd met Carrie Hahn, or since we'd got close, which was only made possible by Deborah's quite silly infidelity with Hoepplewhite. Silly, but another biggish crossing, costing not less than everything. Upon that crossing, Deborah and I no longer were young. Nor Hoepplewhite, who before had been a chesty sort of rumbustious striver, not a full-out villain. Well, off to jail with him now...

Carrie was still young. That was not her hold on me, nor would I take that youth from her before its time. Child-rearing and the demands of the estate would do so, in proper season. It was satisfaction, not sacrifice, to know I would pay any price to be with Carrie. Often people live very long and never know.

THE CHESTERFIELD HOURS

I'd spent just one night in hospital, but it was enough to make me guilty both about Daisy and the house I was selling to strangers. I walked the dog long and often, and tidied up as best I could with my one good arm. The weird long Friday passed, the sun shimmering down as the metropolis emptied out, everybody outward-bound to the mountains or sea-shore, fleeing before the steel canyons fell all under shadow.

I was headed against this exodus into the canyons, into a void actually, as there was no happy hour crowd this holiday Friday when I left at 6:30. Jack and Deborah and the strange-named executor would meet me in a high office.

Since my hospitalization, Daisy had not left my side. She had missed me that night, of course, but she further sensed my vulnerability and pain. Hence I took her with me in the car to the reading. She, for the matter of it, was all in too.

She'd be in comfort, the day being atypically cool, and I parked easily in the shaded, deserted city, leaving her with treats and cracked windows.

The great building, on one of the year's longest days, was plashed with sun at the peak as a dagger's blade with blood, while the earth-bound hilt was darkened. Inside, the security man told me the floor and pointed me to the correct elevator.

This is not my city, I thought, as I rode upwards alone. It was Deborah's, who worked as a paralegal for a downtown law firm. Even in our passionate early days, I now recalled, she would recount the endless proposals and propositions she parried, repelled and possibly considered from partnered movers and would-be shakers. Had those all dried up? Not likely...

254

THE CHESTERFIELD HOURS

I gave a polite rap at the appointed office door, swung it open, and entered. The receptionist's desk of course was unoccupied, so I moved inwards toward a strange raspy voice that called, "Komm een, komm een."

In a corner office round a glass table sat Jack, Deborah, and... well, the strange raspy-voice man. He was oldish, with grey translucent frames over his eyes. His hair was gray and thinned, his mouth wide and satchel-like with thick lips. He wore a Scottish tweed jacket and bow tie. Withal he had an anciently wise if catfishy look. He did not introduce himself, instead waited for Jack –

"Son, this is Mister Treevis -- "

-- to mangle his name, then raised a polite hand to halt the massacre. "Monsieur Chesterfield, 'allo, 'allo, I am Alaistre Treves-Alsace, solicitor and executor for your dear muzzer. Please to sit down."

I sat and looked to the ones I knew. Deborah was dressed more tastefully than I'd seen her in months; that is to say, she had come from work. She glared at me as if I should be made to pay... but we were both beyond that.

My father wore a light navy jacket and shirt with open collar. As to expression, his seemed to indicate that he could not win. Yet the actual truth, I felt, was that the Captain could not lose.

If against all nature there proved to be a Fortune, then it would be Jack's. But there was no Fortune. Jack had always been happy on a Marine's pay and pension. And, severed as he now was from Deborah, nothing could be beguiled of him...

Yet here was Deborah anyway. The strange man picked up the papers in front of him.

"Eh bien."

THE CHESTERFIELD HOURS

We sat, within this great pointed structure, at the juncture of its blade and hilt. Bright sun poured through the top windows and cast only the crowns of four heads into shadows on the wall. The more massive shadow of the room's lower half crept upwards, like a blot, with each ticking second sponging up the light, eating it...

The executor, now all in shade, pulled his great catfish lips into a little smile.

"Madame Ffoulkes Chesterfield, in her instructions to Captain and young Monsieur Chesterfield has, how you say, her own *mode inimitable?*"

Deborah, I noticed, minutely grimaced at this, her eyelids pulsing in a little squint. Jack just stared ahead as if to face the music.

"'To my 'usband John Chesterfield,'" the solicitor read in a raspy drone that was not unmusical, "'I leave my whole library of books. It is never too late, and it is high time. I don't ask that you do Trollope's entire Barsetshire or Palliser series. A little Mark Twain will do nicely for a start. Try stopping Mechanics Illustrated and Sports Illustrated for a year and see what ensues. You always said a man can learn a lot in the w.c. 'ere is your chance to prove eet. I know my son loves my library but it will come to him in time. I am not yet finished with his father's education.'"

Jack Chesterfield too was all in shadow now. He nodded acceptance without emotion. Deborah, bisected with sun and shadow, sat stone-faced looking down. Through the glass table I saw one of her hands tapping her knee.

Treves-Alsace switched on a desk lamp. His face lit up, with only his eyes still greyed over by the spectacle frames. I thought I heard something rustle, but no one spoke for a moment. The air conditioning almost imperceptibly hummed.

The executor stretched his great mouth at Jack.

"The late Madame always must 'ave her fun." He looked down again at his papers.

"'My remaining possessions,'" he read, "'you either have already or are not worth a feeg. Do with them what you will.'"

With a flourish he put aside the printed page. Another page, however, remained.

Yet there was already shifting within the room. Could there really be *so* little? For my part I marveled at the tidiness of it. Jack sighed, apparently, with relief. Deborah did not sigh. Her jaw worked almost grindingly.

The strange man, with another flourish of a delicate hand, picked up the next sheet.

"Ah then. What af we 'ere?"

Tink-a-link...

Startled upright by this sound, I scanned the room. In a shadowy corner by the coat rack wavered the familiar bluish form. The whisky glass took definition.

Good God, I thought, my mother's here.

"You bet I'm here, sonny. I wouldn't miss it." But no one else noticed, not even Jack.

It seemed ruddy telepathy. But the ghostly form also seemed actually to speak as before. I heard the ice clink as she tipped the glass to sip – yet no one else heard or saw a thing.

Treves-Alsace began again to read. "'For my son I 'ave nothing.'"

At this even Jack betrayed an intake of breath. Deborah seemed agitated by... what? Disbelief, anti-climax, good and bad years alike blown hereby to heaven?

I found myself smiling.

"'I would, were it in my power,'" the executor continued, "'give eem the world. But I haven't got it, or much of anything, as by now you know.'"

"Too true," said the voice which only I seemed to hear.

Wait a minute, I thought. It's not just my hearing Mother. Did she not also, a minute ago, answer my mere thoughts?

"Go ahead and speak those thoughts, dear. So long as you address me directly, 'twill stay between us."

Daphne, in her corner, seemed more than normally thirsty today, and tipped her glass for a deep swallow.

Hmm, I thought.

"Just try a little test, dear. Something safe."

"Well," I spoke to the ghost, "I'm satisfied."

Satisfied to get nothing, with the end of Fortune talk. It would pass for a valedictory to the group...

...but no one at the table reacted to my utterance.

"D'you see, dear? It works."

Treves-Alsace resumed reading. "'There is something that passes down to males in the Ffoulkes line. It has never touched me, as I like my mother was an only child. Swifty -- '" he looked up and smiled. "C'est moi, un sobriquet," he said, and went back to his text -- "'Swifty has taken good care of it over many years, and will put you in the picture.'"

"Passes down to Ffoulkes males," I repeated numbly, addressing Daphne's ghost, who shook her glass as if prospecting for a last half-dram of bourbon. "That's sounds almost like -- "

"Right, dear, it's a sort of entail."

"Entailment! Good God, Mother, Henry the Eighth and Norman Mailer think that's a patriarchal atrocity."

"One many Ffoulkes women have thrived by, dear. Not ones, however, who marry American soldiers."

Daphne started crunching her bourbony ice-bits, something I hadn't seen her do since she was alive.

I turned back to the main action. Jack was puzzledly cogitating. Deborah's eyes were wide and furious.

Swifty continued:

"'In the old days, land was first and money behind. Land for social status, land for power, land for entail. Well, as I understand it, the Ffoulkes family rather shrewdly caught the modern turning point. Thereby were liquidated glorious uplands, hunt country with fishing rights, rich farmland with generational tenants, and yes, productive mines and factories. All liquidated, but to this day well-husbanded, if capital can be analogized with God's earth. And I'm not sure it decently can be. But Swifty will have it. Do be a good Ffoulkes son and put a bit of it back into the land.'"

"Voila." Swifty handed me the paper.

As I dazedly stared at the figures beneath Daphne's instructions, I thought I heard my mother mutter something that died out to nothing. But I kept my eyes on the paper.

Rather spread about, it was. Much of it in British banks, of course, but also in Swiss, and German, and French, and American, even Irish and Spanish. Mostly in euros, portions in sterling and dollars. With goggling eyes I did a hasty job of addition. It looked cutting up close to nine figures...

"Mother," I said out of the corner of my mouth as I studied, "how came you to be so indiscreet about The Fortune to Deborah on the eve of our wedding, when you never said a word to me in thirty-two years?"

There was no reply, but in the corner of my eye I saw Deborah's head snap toward me. I looked to the coat rack, but no one, nothing was there.

"Son?" Jack said.

"He's... he's talking to his mother!" Deborah said. "About me! He's out of his mind!"

Swifty Treves-Alsace removed his tinted glasses to reveal twinkling brown eyes under salt and pepper brows.

"Finis," he said. "You 'ave my number, and I am at your disposal, Monsieur."

I felt blood rushing to my face. I put the paper inside my jacket.

"He deceived me," Deborah said, "and he's crazy to boot!"

Swifty stood and made a courtly bow. "C'est tres difficile, Mademoiselle – ou Madame? – to be the one thing and to do the other. Au revoir, Madamoiselle et Messieurs."

In a bursting sweat I looked back to the coat rack. The bluish figure stood there with a full glass. The words stuck in my mouth...

"Mm... Moth... Mother, for the love of God! What have you done to me?"

The others in the room did not react.

Daphne calmly sipped. "I stepped out to fix a fresh drink. I hope you didn't speak indiscreetly, dear."

"They heard me! You said if I addressed you directly they wouldn't."

"Well, I wasn't present to be addressed, now was I?"

Deborah badgered the retreating Swifty.

"Did you know he caused a riot just this week in a downtown gym? Another riot he caused in a restaurant over the winter." Her trump card to the Gallic solicitor: "A *French* restaurant! He's not competent!"

Swifty, briefcase in hand, swept from the room with a little wave. Deborah followed him to the door, Jack reaching to her from behind.

I carefully and severely spoke toward the coat rack. "I say, Mother, it's a bit pushing it, when our Provvy is sporting enough to allow you three whiskies a day already."

Daphne just took it in her stride and sipped. "I'm thirsty, sonny, and this is a gala day."

"It's a very old joke, Mother, but a gal a day is about all I can handle, especially when she's pissed on four Manhattans."

I walked out the office door and into the reception area. Deborah was yelling something to Swifty as the solicitor disappeared down the hall.

Jack gently took her by the elbow. "Now, now, be a good sport, sweetie. Look at me."

She turned and slammed him with the flat of her hand on the chest.

"Don't ever touch me again, you old slob!"

She might have remembered the Captain was mere days out of hospital for the ticker beneath that breastbone.

I walked up and put an arm round my father's shoulders. The three of us shifted about uneasily by the outer office doorway. At that moment a tall, blonde-haired man in a suit walked up the hallway toward us, carrying a briefcase. Deborah's furious expression faded.

"Oh, hello, Rex," she said, come-hitherishly. "What are you doing here on a holiday weekend?"

The new chap was thirty-fiveish, blue-eyed with very shiny shoes.

"Deborah!" he said in some surprise.

Then, in what I thought sounded suspiciously like script, he said, "They say I'm a cinch for partner, but I'm taking nothing for granted, you know?"

There are persons, I knew, who seem to have been selling themselves since kindergarten. A chosen few find always and only a buyers' market – as Rex did now...

"Well, geez," Deborah said fondishly, "you gotta have some fun in life."

There was a crack of space through the doorway. The guv'nor and I locked eyes, and Jack lifted his brows. On soft cat's feet, the two-hundred pound Captain glided out into the hallway, the leaner son hot-foot behind him.

The elevator opened.

Deborah was saying to Rex, "Did you ever watch the fireworks from the top of this building?"

The Captain and I caught the elevator as a maintenance man emerged.

"You can lock up 1218 now," I told the fellow.

On the way down, Jack merely said, "Well."

"Right," I replied.

It was the bulliest conversation of the day. And so did we part on the street, me saying only, "Catch you up tomorrow, Dad."

"Check."

Daisy was resting easy in the back seat of the darkened car. I got in, reached back, and stroked her.

"Some changes coming, Daisy. But just you keep your head on straight, old girl. No great gaudy awful necklaces for you, hear?"

Once home, I had a small brandy, then took dog and book to bed with me.

IT'LL COST YOU

Shemp Hahn, I learned when I called next day, hadn't got round yet to deeding the estate to Carrie. This was the result, Shemp said with some irritation, of my making such a shtunk back in the metrop that everything got set back.

"It's splendid to hear you using the colorful ethnic vernacular of old, sir. It can only mean you're getting out of the country land-owner business."

"How's that?" Shemp said a bit warily.

"I'll pay you five million cash for the estate. Top dollar, no financing, clean as a whistle, sir. Can't do better."

"What about my vineyards and stables?"

"What about two-fifty K per annum for the rights?"

"Ooowwh! What am I, a pigeon?"

"I believe, sir, and it will doubtless be coming back to you, that the saying goes, 'What am I, a schmuck?' And the answer would be no, you wouldn't be. With five million in hand, and your very considerable income from grape sales to local wineries, and the growing brand value of your own boutique winery, and your connections to Finger Lakes Race Track, you'd be doing very well indeed. With every incentive to maintain your entrepreneurial edge."

"I'll think it over."

THE CHESTERFIELD HOURS

I played my hole card. "And of course Carrie and I want you and Mrs. Hahn to stay living on the estate."

Thereby was the deal done. And I stand by the lesson. For happy ever-aftering, friend reader, be not afraid to spend both love and fortune.

TIME PASSES

GOODNIGHT, ALL

I wish for every friend reader that she should consummate her marriage above a crystalline northern lake in early autumn; that she and her beloved should be embowered in a country stable, with the sweet smell of fresh-mown hay, spiced with wood smoke from the great house, riding in on lake breezes through the screens. She will have walked with, then been carried by her beloved past the nodding thoroughbred horses who will stand staunch as supporting beams beneath the lovemaking that starts with a caress and grows continually more vigorous...

The old twin beds of course will have been replaced by a king, that of her mother and father who will sleep on it again and hereafter...

Carrie and I were each in light flannel, I in standard pyjamas, she in a nightie that ended a bit above the knee. We would be needing the flannels as we and the long night cooled down together. But we were not there yet.

The dogs were in the great house, and rather in a snit about it. Perhaps they would be fetched back here later... perhaps not.

This same day, back in the metrop, Larry and Jeanine had had their first wedding ceremony at St. Casimir's Catholic Church. On the morrow, the new Chesterfields and the elder Hahns would travel down by limo to the Jewish ceremony put on by Larry's parents. It was agreeable, if a bit tiring...

But that was tomorrow. For this night of nights, Carrie and I were well rested. We had not drunk over-much, and we even had done great long separate dog-walks in the morning before the ceremony at St. John's. As we lay now in the huge bed, we were quite fully alive in the senses.

Husband, gently with his thumb, drew aside wife's forelock bang, caressing her temple, and kissed her on the mouth. Her hands encircled my neck and locked behind it.

The bed was like a football pitch. One might do anything upon it. The new sheets were cool and fragrant.

"Well," I said.

"Well," she said, the lashes dropping over her green oval eyes.

Tink-a-link...

We lovers sat up sharpish. Carrie folded both legs under her.

"I say, really now, Mother, eh what?"

We looked to the window corner by the curtains. But there was no definite female form or whisky glass, just a sort of bluish haze that joined with the night. Yet the voice came clear enough.

"Do carry on, children. I'm not even here."

THE END

Page past GP's photo for a preview of the first Chesterfield and Carrie Finger Lakes mystery:

THE CHESTERFIELD CLUE

Coming from Gwyn Parry and Once Upon Avon Press!

Gwyn Parry is Welsh, German, American, and something else or other. He lives, a bit less grandly than Chesterfield and Carrie, in the Finger Lakes wine country. Tell him what you're reading, or ask him anything at www.thegwynparryhours.com

From THE CHESTERFIELD CLUE

The first Chesterfield and Carrie mystery:

UNDER HEAVEN

Too much of joy. Carrie and I, beneath that blue sky, above that bluer lake, knew no blue times. No shame, night after night in our marriage bed, nor hard gray mornings. Our bodies still young and bold, yet all green-sickness gone of youth. We were completed in each other.

Our happy ending by now you know. Legion friend readers have sung it as satisfying, just, well-earned, etc. Legion friend readers also have made visits to West Lake Road. And because rich, poor and middling they are the best of souls, they are well met here with tea, scones, and even Riesling. Shemp Hahn's Riesling, naturally, the cold climate specialty of our Finger Lakes wineries. Red vinifera grapes, especially here above Canandaigua Lake, have always been chancey.

My roguish father-in-law, though, was busy playing against Nature. With five million iron men from me in the bank, he set to making a red wine that would *schneider* the critics but good. Thereby hangs a sad tale. Human nature is a darkness. There is no Paradise under blue or any skies, in this our life on earth.

***

"Double Gold cannot be done. Not in reds, my friend. Not up here."

"Don't doubt me." As he said this, Shemp Hahn struck his glass against that of his boyhood chum, Morris Farber. To myself, standing six feet from them, this "toast" conveyed an ominous aggression, less a fraternal clink than a violent *clank!*, something out of Tubular Bells in "The Exorcist."

"Father!" Carrie burst out.

My wife is no alarmist. The two men's glasses might have shattered. Standing with Carrie in our large piano parlor, I noticed dark little blotches that flecked the jacket lapels and white shirt of Morris Farber. Shemp Hahn displayed his wolfish predator's grin. Farber, much the shorter and rounder, for that matter much the balder, for an instant looked like a baby who'd surprised himself with mystery bubbles in the bathtub. Then he roared with laughter.

"So touchy, this one!" he said. "You tell the man a fact of reality, and suddenly already he's all over you like the old Brooklyn Shmuely!"

"He's just a big baby, is what he is," said Carrie, as she stepped in with a cloth napkin dipped in the water pitcher. "Here, Uncle Mo, let me dab those stains before they set. And we're sending out this shirt and jacket on Father's tab, because I won't have either you or Juanita troubled with them."

Mo Farber had his hands lightly on his goddaughter's ribs. "Sweetheart, you're the best. Only his darling daughter does he love, but don't worry, he always listens to Morris, because from wine, Morris Farber knows."

Carrie's mother Barbara, stunning in a burgundy winter dress and black heels, was moving like love's revenge across the room, trailed by Captain Jack Chesterfield.

"Bull---," Shemp Hahn said, measuring that faintly vicious grin. "Morris talks and talks, but in the end he's the one takes the lesson, don't you, Moey?"

Where was I, Chesterfield, at this point? Merely watching, listening, holding a glass of Mo Farber's Silver-winning Cabernet Franc. And thinking how strange all this was to see and hear.

Only his daughter does he love?

"What silliness is this?" Barbara Hahn asked in that warm, cultured, erotic voice that thrills at least two generations I know still to have blood in them. Such as, my own and my father's.

"Everything okay here?" said my guv'nor the Captain, who's always on duty in some sense or other. He was the only one drinking beer, which marked him out to me as his own man, to wine snobs as perhaps a too common one...

(And have I made explicit that my widowed father now lives on the estate, in the apartment over the stables that my in-laws speedily abandoned for a rear wing of the big house?)

"Everything's beauty-ful," Shemp said, turning to his wife, giving a contemptuous flick of the head toward Jack. "Sergeant Yawk here can stand down, and have another six-pack."

"And you can just have a cigar, my dear," said Barbara with the smoky steel in her voice of a fine bourbon. Take it outside, in other words.

Except for Morris, we men were all six-foot or better, all fit in our own fashions. I was in my own house, and lest Shemp Hahn forget it, I acted friendlily but firmly to re-master it.

"Let's to the gallery," I said. "Shemp's cigars and Mo's Cab Franc sound just the ticket."

"You go have a good smoke, son," Captain Jack said. He, in other words, would do his own act of defusion by staying back. For ultimately, this decorated warrior was that strongest of things, a man of peace.

Shemp Hahn had no choice really but to adjourn honorably. Morris Farber, a zestful man of appetites, his jacket gone, delightedly threw a shirt-sleeved arm upwards around his old pal's neck.

"Fresh glasses, Juanita," he called. "And full!"

I'd paid Juanita two-hundred dollars just to be here this night, not to labor much after her normal day, just to be a comforting presence, to do what she knew to do if necessary. I was working up to doing something much more for her. I mean, if I tried I couldn't spend it all...

We moved out onto the darkened gallery which overlooked the frozen lake and was level with the huge rising moon. It was not terribly cold for January, and Morris at least was sweating anyway. I'm not sure Shemp ever did.

Shemp did not like to waste his fine cigars, and I gave him a subtle sign that he needn't, this time, on me. The two older men passed a cutting tool between them which Shemp then pocketed. They used a silver lighter, and blew great plumes of smoke. Morris directly took a gulp of his own dark wine, as if it were the climax in a chained sensory ritual. Shemp coolly abstained for now. In fact, his glass was carelessly set on the railing.

"I do believe," I ventured, "that you fellows talking wine is the only sort of argument I care to hear. I feel that I'm learning the story of my own soil."

"Your soil," Shemp said a snide croak, punctuated with a dry little cigar spit. "What I'm paying you, you don't have to learn nothing. I wish somebody paid me a quarter mil, back when, not to go to school."

"Don't mind him," Morris said to me. "You got just the right mind-set. If I was you, I'd enjoy the drinking, and leave the headaches to us. Don't go into the business!"

"I won't, Mo. You labor that we may delectate."

"It's my honor," he said with a catch of emotion, "to provide joy and good times like tonight to people who appreciate. There are no strangers who drink my wines."

Shemp just drew on his cigar.

Morris lifted the bottle itself, as if it were Excaliber. "This symbolizes our struggle. To Silver in international competition is a staggering achievement for a local red wine. Blood, sweat and tears, my friend. And nobody appreciates, except fine young people like you and Carrie."

"He don't talk about his Riesling," Shemp said. "Which proves my point exactly."

I Chesterfield, new to the region, didn't quite grasp the point or the original argument. I knew Farber Estates Winery was on the west shore of Keuka, the more temperate, wishbone-shaped Finger Lake to our southeast.

"My Riesling speaks for itself," Mo said. "It's gotten two Golds, and two Silvers when the season stunk. It's in every restaurant, unlike our friend's here."

"One entry for me in Riesling, and one Gold. Been there, done that."

Mo Farber turned less mirthful. "You ain't done Double Gold, which is gettable in Riesling, for you like it is for me. And I ain't quit trying."

He turned to me and said, "Don't forget that Captain A-rab actually did kill the White Whale. Obsession can take you a long way, if you know your business."

Now back to Shemp, he said, "Riesling is a white whale we can kill. But Cab Sauv, up here, is craziness. You always been a bastard, but never crazy till now."

Shemp Hahn just puffed his cigar and stared at the moon over the lake. I was for shifting the subject.

"Well, I know but a little, but I hear 'em talking up Cab Franc as the new signature wine of the Finger Lakes. It's red, it pleases, and Mo's already Silvered with it. Why not, Shemp, ride Cab Franc for all it's worth?"

"Because it's peasant wine," my father-in-law said to the lake and sky. And for once in a lifetime, and to make a nasty point, he wasted a cigar by dropping it into the glass on the railing, filled with Mo Farber's Cab Franc which he hadn't deigned to taste.

***

Shemp walked back into the house. Morris Farber bent over sighing, head downcast, with both hands on the railing. For a fleeting moment he looked piteously defeated. Then he looked up, and I saw, in the bluish night, his broad smile.

"That one! Like he don't come from peasants, same as me?"

He was a lovely man. It was only my second or third time around Morris Farber, but this night I really first gathered his love of life, of vocation, of family and of all the world. Instinctively, without forethought, I put a hand on his shoulder.

"Cutting off his nose, and all that," I said. "Spoiling his own Havana in your fine wine. Well, who needs him, with a house full of spectacular women a-waiting on us?"

And smiling myself to show no real malice toward Shemp Hahn, I moved us to rejoin the party.

Directly there was a crash, and a shout. I could I suppose give you the full Jane Austen descriptive treatment of this party, the drama of a lifted eyebrow, who sits with whom and why, the subtle patrilineal war, etc. Perhaps I could, but we were fully in a 21st century hot zone here...

"Ya butterfingers moron! Lookit 'at!"

Gee, wonder who said that. A young man in a white jacket, with medium-dark skin and glossy black hair, stood helpless with an empty tray in hand, a shattered glass and a puddle of Shemp's Riesling on the hardwood by his shoes.

Juanita swept across the room more like Sharapova than the fiftyish matron she was.

"Ah, Miguel," she clucked, a towel in hand, bending with and dropping it over glass and liquid. "Is too soon, too soon."

"Get him the f--- outta here," Shemp Hahn snarled, the old Brooklyn accent that years had muted now bared again like fangs.

277

THE CHESTERFIELD HOURS

It was a horrid spectacle. I did not like to see Juanita so bent, as I had not liked to see Mo Farber bent, even for a second, in defeat. The young man was not butter-fingered; he was effectively three-fingered. He was Army Corporal Miguel "Mike" Torrez, decorated and honorably discharged with wounds from Afghanistan. I had only just met him...

Carrie was pulling Juanita up almost into an embrace. Barbara Hahn, who could *really* sweep 'cross a room, came up on her rabid husband.

"Enough!" she said. And here I stepped in, though it seemed but yesterday that my mother-in-law actually did, with regal grace, rule this house.

"Right, then. You will retire, Shemp. Goodnight."

Through all the tumult two figures kept stone rigid. The two soldiers, Miguel and Captain Jack, stood erect, drilling their eyes at Shemp Hahn.

"Come on, Miggy," said Carrie, who'd known the young man most of their lives. She discarded the tray and took him by his good hand into the kitchen.

Barbara's hand was on her husband's chest. Shemp roughly backhanded it off. My father's jaw worked furiously; I had not seen him like this. Both older men were tall, vigorous, powerful: Shemp in a Downtown Athletic Club squash champion sort of a way; Captain Jack in a kill-ten-VC-with-a-trench-knife sort of way...

"I'll just see to that young lad," said the man of peace my guv'nor, and took himself off to join Carrie and Miggy/Mike. I thought I might have seen his hand graze Barbara's as he went. Chivalry, maybe...

THE CHESTERFIELD HOURS

I had not moved, nor emoted in any way since my utterance. I was at my full height. Shemp would withdraw, and I would exert nary muscle, only my authority over him and the estate.

Barbara went to the gallery door and opened it. She said to me:

"Thank you for dismissing this lout, my husband, from our gathering. Will you honor my wish that he leave the premises entirely?"

I skimmed a look across Shemp Hahn. This was to acknowledge him in the barest, most contemptuous way.

"Of course he goes, madame, this minute. Until you say the word, he only returns daytimes, to labor as an outdoors tenant." Loved saying that – peasant indeed!

A gray cat walked in the open door. It was a stranger to us all…

"Kiss my a--, Lord Fauntleroy!"

Morris Farber floated up to Shemp's side. "Come on, Shmuely. We'll go to town for a brandy."

The vitality of his love was inextinguishable. The two old Brooklyn friends went out, and I shut the door behind them.

Nothing occurred now but to look at the cat, which wandered our midst as if it owned the place. It was full-bodied, mature, lustrously groomed. We hadn't a neighbor within half a mile. Any strange cat here should be feral, and coyote food soon as the sun set…

My corgi Daisy walked up curiously, and the cat rubbed against her from their muzzles down to their tails. Carrie's big yellow lab Cyrus, friendly but a bruiser, loomed up and got biffed in the nose for his trouble. The cat then sat, and its almond eyes went half shut.

Carrie emerged alone from the kitchen and went to her mother's side. Soon as she saw the cat, with a little cry of delight she swooped it up

279

in her arms. The cat "went with it," as the young people say, and allowed itself to be cradled baby-like in my wife's arms. From some feet away I could hear it purr.

"What a big girl," Carrie cooed. "Where'd you come from?"

Not to beat into the ground my master of the house bit, but I spoke to this latest. "I'll not chuck her out, love. Not on a winter night, and not as she's already on terms all round."

Carrie gently turned the cat and danced her on Cyrus' brawny back. Maybe it was my love's touch, but both animals now seemed fully in the spirit.

I saw Barbara Hahn look towards the kitchen. Juanita was in there now as well...

It gave me a push across the room, and I took one step into the kitchen. Juanita was at the sink, with her back to the two men. My father and Miggy Mike stood facing close together. Captain Jack had the young man's mangled right hand in his own; the older man's other hand cradled Miggy Mike's face.

I had lived a lifetime without such a moment with my father. I stood outside myself for a moment. Then I withdrew.

No, I never gave you the full Austen on this party, and too late now, as it dissolved utterly after Shemp's little snit. There'd been perhaps 20 people, mainly lake, wine, and other friends of Shemp and Barbara. Off they went, forcing cheer as they retreated.

My father emerged alone, with a fresh beer, and sat in a chair against the wall. The chair had a near neighbor, and I dropped into it.

"Mmm," the Captain said.

"Right," I said. Some of our best conversations took this tenor. There is a strong case for minimalism.

The gray cat sauntered up, gathered its bulk an instant, leapt and settled in Captain Jack's lap. Automatically he stroked it, and directly the cat was doing that love-kneading thing on the old boy's winter slacks, unavoidably in a sensitive spot.

Like a gentleman, the guv'nor just discreetly shifted. Like a gentleman, I just tactfully looked off. Like a very demon, the cat continued to "go to town," as they say.

Barbara Hahn, out of whatever motive, picked this moment to brighten from her enervations. "Puss puss!" she said, and reached out. "What's your name, Puss?"

In a flash, the cat raked Barbara's lovely hand with its claws. I saw a white flap of skin and a ribbon of blood.

"We'll call her Peevish," I said, and rose. "I'll just fix her some dog food, light cream, and a litterbox of Basmati rice, as it looks like she'll be staying."

Collectively, we'd all had it. Done in, you know. People just streamed away, as I completed my humble task. The dogs dashed to their beds upstairs. I never saw Juanita leave with Miggy Mike, nor the cat follow my father out to the stables, past the horses, and up into his loft...

Next I was upstairs in the bedroom with Carrie. What she was feeling, I had no idea, and I was roiled myself by thoughts and emotions from the evening, which I couldn't bring to sense or closure.

The bath off our bedroom was Carrie's, and she came from it in a calf-length robe, bare feet, and fresh scrubbed face. Eros was strong with us always up here. Yet I wanted beyond all else simply to clutch her to me, feel her warmth, release this nameless unrest.

She came near, smiling, fresh, untroubled. Somehow I couldn't reach for her.

"I... I... "

She put a fingertip to my lips.

"We're going to have a baby," she said.

The past silly night of broken glass, of soggy cigars and strange beasts went straight to oblivion. The future was saved, there was only the future, the future...